Pieceworks

PIECEWORKS

Jeanette Reid

Faraway Publishing
Black Mountain, N.C.

The author may be contacted at
62 Wagon Trail
Givens Highland Farms
200 Tabernacle Road
Black Mountain, NC 28711

Cover photograph by Ernest Jahnke.

With deep appreciation to Murray Johnston for her fiber art quilt,
which has hung on the wall of my study and inspired me for many years.

Published by
FARAWAY PUBLISHING
125 Spring View Drive
Black Mountain, N.C. 28711

Printed in the United States of America

ISBN: 978-0-9710130-8-7

Library of Congress Control Number: 2023936230

DEDICATION

To the wonderful teachers I have had (both prose & poetry) in the *Great Smokies Writing Program*: Peggy Millin, Cathy Smith Bowers, Tina Barr, & Elizabeth Lutyens for their keen critiques and supportive encouragement.

Thanks to Randolph Shaffner for his guidance and expertise in publishing, without which this book would not exist.

Special thanks to my husband, Judd Redfield, for his helpful listening and ongoing support.

I am also grateful to my storytelling family as we sat around the Sunday dinner table in my small West Tennessee town and heard tale after tale going back for several generations.

CONTENTS

PIECEWORK 1

MRS. FERRY 131

THE LOVE SEAT 141

RIDING THE PIPPIN 153

JAPANESE FAN... 165

BYRON PATE 173

INTRODUCTION

Jeanette Reid is a consummate poet and engaging storyteller. Her poetry sparkles with bright and clever images, the intertwining of nostalgia and good humor, and a deep appreciation of both nature and humankind. Her prose, like her poetry, is more poetic than plain. Her Decembers are so cold and bitter that "the stubble in the field sparkles with frost, and the cows stand close to each other blowing out their steamy breath." If eyes are green, they are "clear green, like Coke bottle glass." If the night is dark, it's "hidden in blackness, obscure as the mouth of a cave whose dark passages wind blindly into the unknown." A cabin in the midst of a clearing is made visible by the "sun streaming down toward the porch creating a well of light in the dark woods." The legs of an overturned love seat are "sticking up in the air like a donkey," and the stare of a domineering adult is "like a magnet, a huge white moon, so fixed and enormous" that a child is compelled to look even while cringing away.

The beauty of Reid's style is reflected in the subtle development of her characters, mostly youth trying to see and understand the outer world and find deeper meaning within their own lives. Sixteen-year-old Norma Jean Taylor desperately seeks answers to the questions that have plagued her since she discovered a miniature quilt under a false bottom of an old chest in the attic of the family farm. Ninety-year-old Avis relives her early years with the rediscovery of a delicate Japanese fan in the bottom of a Malaysian teak chest. A gas mask, a ration box, and a roller coaster indelibly link a fourth grader to her great Uncle Fan's double life as a hell-raiser and chastened veteran of the Great War. And when a middle-school girl befriends a painfully reclusive classmate, it's a black upright piano that opens up new worlds filled with joy.

Reid's narrative turns hilarious when a shy third grader meets her nemesis in the terrifying guise of a server in the school cafeteria. And when a young couple discovers a discarded love seat in the middle of a highway and involves the whole family in a spirited debate about what to do with it, Reid shows a rare mastery of local lingo, absurd situations, and surprise.

This collection of "Pieceworks" depicts characters of every age from nine to ninety. Its moods range from joy to sorrow, nostalgia, suspense, surprise, frustration, anger, fear, and hilarity. Against the inevitable clash of the outer with the inner world, the unconventional characters in this novella and five short stories emerge as pieces in the freeform design of a beautiful quilt that gives symmetry and deep-rooted meaning to their individual lives. A beautiful read!

Randolph P. Shaffner

Black Mountain, N. C.
March 15, 2023

PIECEWORK

CHAPTER 1

1953

Norma Jean climbs the ladder to the hayloft, pausing when her head clears the opening to inhale the sweet-dry aroma of baled hay. When she was a child, she played up in the loft a lot, she and her friend Shirleen, jumping down the stacked-up bales or making doll towns, each bale a house, a store, or playground. That seems long ago. She hasn't been up here in ages, but the smell, the dust motes floating in the air, the pigeons perched or flapping about in the high open space near the roof feel comforting and familiar.

She walks across the wide floor, mostly empty after the winter's cattle feeding, and stands at the open loft door breathing in the fresh air of spring. This is what's brought her here. The day, bright and clear, opens before her, and the fields newly plowed and greening, the long hedgerows that separate them, the trees along the river. Aunt Edna is hanging up sheets on the clothesline behind the house, and they wave about like living creatures in the light breeze. On the road to town cars pass, getting smaller and smaller in the distance. In the farthest bean field, she can just make out Uncle Frank's tractor inching its way down the rows.

She stands on the level of hawks, crows, and buzzards, and like them, she slowly surveys her territory. One wouldn't miss much of the farm's activities from this view, she thinks. No wonder Uncle Frank stays out here at the barn so much. It's his own place, like the attic is for me—familiar and undisturbed by the activities of others.

She turns toward the opening in the barn floor to descend the ladder. Even now she feels the childhood fear that unnerved her whenever she was about to go down. It's made of short boards nailed into the barn wall. To go down, you have to sit on the side of the open hole, lean over and grasp a slat, then slide forward, legs scrambling to get a foothold. There's always that moment when the hole looks deep and scary, when she's not sure her arms will support her until her feet find their grounding.

Today she hesitates, reaches out for the ladder, slides off the edge. Suddenly, her foot slips just as she's moving her hand down to the next slat. She grabs at the ladder wildly. A splinter jabs her palm as she gains a new foothold. It looks ugly, one end still attached to the ladder. She can't let go with her other hand to pull it out. Holding on tightly, she is trying to calm herself, taking deep breaths when something odd catches her eye, a piece of leather, it seems, pushed in between the loft floor and the wall.

Gritting her teeth, she jerks her hand upward releasing it from the jagged wood. It's too dim here between loft and ground to examine the puncture, but before continuing down, she reaches up for the old piece of leather and is surprised to pull out a thin worn billfold. Strange. She tosses it onto the loft floor, then carefully placing her hands on the ladder, climbs back up.

In the light pouring through the loft door Norma Jean examines her hand. No sign of any splinter left in the wound, but she squeezes to push out more blood, sucks it to relieve the sting. The billfold has slid under some loose straw, and she picks it up, curious, wondering what in the world she has found. She holds it between her two hands, not opening it immediately, but feeling the smoothness of the old leather and speculating on its origin.

Whose could this be? Did Grandpa Travis tuck it away up here, an important paper or money hidden for safekeeping ? She's overheard how he distrusted banks and government offices. Maybe it was hoboes, "drifters" Aunt Edna calls them, who sleep in lofts undetected, and sometimes hide things in barns across the county to retrieve on another visit. Or Uncle Frank could have forgotten he placed it here long ago, perhaps before he and Aunt Edna married.

Warm sunlight pours in on Norma Jean's head, glossing her brown hair. The billfold feels flat, so light she expects it to be empty. And when she opens it up, it *looks* empty at first, no bills or papers. She raises it to her nose and smells the leather. The white edge of something is stuck under a flap on one side. Giving it a tug, she pulls out a photograph, old and yellowing. A young girl looks out from the

4

snapshot, pretty in a delicate way with high cheekbones and a tapering chin. Her lips are closed, but slightly curved from some inner amusement. The eyes look toward the camera, but beyond, beyond the photographer, beyond Norma Jean to some other place, some vision on the distant horizon. Norma Jean is transfixed, hardly breathing. Here she is, sixteen years old, sitting on a bale of hay in the barn loft in the sunlight looking at a picture—she feels sure of it—of her mother.

The young woman in the photo is confident; Norma Jean can see that. Confident and clear-minded in a way the world might call bold, yet natural and unselfconscious, at home with who she is and what she's about. Is it possible to be like this, so free and sure?

She runs her fingers over the photograph. "So this is how you looked, Julia" she says. "But who put your picture here—and why?" There's so much she doesn't know. She looks for some trace of herself in the photograph—the chin perhaps, the shape of the eyes, if not the attitude.

Whatever the reason, it's here for her to find. And maybe it's a sign, a clue that she's about to learn more. She considers taking it with her, hiding it in the attic where she can study the face and feel her mother's presence beside her as she works. But something holds her back. This place seems to be where the picture belongs. Perhaps her mother loved the hayloft, spent happy times here. Whoever hid the billfold certainly thought of her here.

Norma Jean smiles and lightly kisses the young woman's image. She'll think of her here, too; come see her whenever she wants. For now she slips the photo back in its leather case and crosses the loft floor to its secret place, her secret now.

***

Norma Jean glances up at the small group of women sitting around the table in the back room of the church, then looks down again. She's younger than the other women in this quilting circle, younger by fifty years than Miss Ella Mae who's been quilting as long as anyone can remember—wedding quilts, baby quilts, quilts for beds and buggies and walls.

Bea Jones, a distant cousin of Shirleen's, is old enough to be Norma Jean's mother, though she tries to dress younger. Tonight she's wearing hoop earrings and a peasant blouse. She talks the whole time they are quilting, gossip mostly. She's figured out who, what, and where about everybody in Pine Grove.

Ethel Posey sits with them every week, even though she hasn't quilted for a while. The arthritis has taken hold. But Tuesday evenings this is where she's going to be, and her notions of color, size and placement are always true. Sometimes they bring in quilts they've started at home, getting suggestions from each other about fabric and design. Once a quilt face is finished they all help out with the actual quilting, those tiny, even stitches that secure the bright-colored face to the backing. At other times they work together from the start to make a special-occasion quilt for someone in the community.

Norma Jean is glad to be part of this circle even though they're older. She's been quilting most of her young life, and she's comfortable here, sitting around the quilting table, listening to their talk, working with the material. More comfortable by far than sitting at the cafeteria table in high school where everyone vies for attention as she tries to become invisible. Her pale skin and quiet nature help her disappear.

These women have among them a lot of experience, a wealth of wisdom, and she has some questions, troubling questions about her family she can't ask at home. Finding the photograph has whetted her long-held desire to learn more about her mother and grandfather, but she knows she must be careful. Pine Grove is small, and most people tend to mind their own business. Put the wrong way, her queries could make them withdraw into their quilting, cautious and silent.

She chooses her words carefully like she makes her stitches, waiting until she has just the right spot to poke in her needle and noticing already, as she pulls through the thread, whether or not she has missed the mark.

"I wonder," she says, as casually as she can, "I wonder where all these scraps of cloth we use come from. I mean, I know they come from different folks' scrap bags, but lots of them I don't recognize. I always notice what people are wearing, the material I mean, but this piece here, for example"—she nods at a piece she is working with, a bright blue background with little daisies that seem to be dancing—"I've never seen this being worn by anybody around here."

Bea Jones looks up with a snort. "Well, honey, you only *been* around here for the whole of your sixteen years, and for most of those you was just a child. The material in these bags goes back a lot further than that."

"That was a Sunday dress of Annie Yates," declares Miss Ella Mae. "Looked pretty on her, too." She pauses. "But after she had her twins, you know, and her husband took off, I never saw her wear it again."

Annie Yates has been dead for at least five years. Norma Jean remembers the slight, sad-looking little woman and can't begin to picture her in a dress of dancing daisies.

"The other day," Ethel says, nodding and smiling brightly at Norma Jean, "I was going through some old scrap bags looking for good colors for the wedding quilt we'll start soon for the Hadleys, and I swear I saw a piece from a shirt your grandpa Travis, used to wear. Must have been his favorite, he wore it most every Sunday."

Her grandpa. She'd never even known him.

"What was he like?" she asked, seeing her opening. "Was he anything like Uncle Frank?"

The quilters look up in surprise as though they don't know how to answer. "Well," says Ethel, "they both worked the farm; still, everybody's different. We're moving slow tonight with all this yakking. Better get back to what we're here for."

Norma Jean picks up her needle, and wonders whether anyone would tell her if a piece of fabric came out of the bag from a dress that her mother wore. If only the photograph of her had been large enough to show her dress or blouse.

***

As soon as she gets home, Norma Jean heads for the attic. Home is an old two-story farmhouse three miles from town, the Taylor place, where she lives with Aunt Edna, Uncle Frank, and Gram. Taylor men have farmed this land for three generations; her grandfather, the last to do so, died the year before she was born. Her mother, Julia, his youngest daughter, drowned a year later. A bad time for her family. But the details are a big mystery to Norma Jean. In their household no one will talk about it. The past is a closed subject.

Lucky for her though, her tiny bedroom at the end of the upstairs hall has access to the attic, narrow steps inside the closet that curve up to a door. Uncle Frank says the steps were always there, they'd just walled off part of the hallway to make the extra room needed when she came along. Norma Jean doesn't mind that it's small; she likes the cozy feeling and the double windows that look west across the peach trees, barn lot, and green fields beyond. But most of all, she likes going up those narrow steps into the spaciousness of the big dusty attic.

This is where she finds family, in discarded furniture, trunks of old clothing, boxes of the stuff of past generations. But no pictures. She's looked all over the attic. Not a one, here or below. Until last week in the hayloft, she'd never seen a picture of her mother. When she'd asked several years ago where some family pictures were, Aunt Edna said they upset Gram, so she'd taken them all away.

Gram had a stroke right after Julia died, and Aunt Edna made up her mind they would close the door on the past. When Norma Jean asked where she'd taken them, Aunt Edna put her hands on her hips and took a breath of exasperation.

"Forget those old pictures, Norma Jean. I don't want to hear about them anymore. Just picture *this* instead: half my family dead in a year's time; you a baby, and Mama a very sick woman, to care for. We

8

couldn't even say Julia's or Daddy's name without her getting all agitated."

Aunt Edna had grabbed her dishrag and started scouring the kitchen sink. "We got enough to tend to right here today without dragging in the past. Won't change a thing, and could cause a lot of harm. Those folks are dead and gone now." She'd looked at Norma Jean over the top of her glasses.

"Be glad you're here, Norma Jean, with us to take care of you. Your job is to tend to what's on your own doorstep. Seems like a lesson some folks just never learn."

Aunt Edna is a thickset woman with broad shoulders and sturdy legs. She keeps her dark hair in a tight perm that circles a face whose most prominent feature is eyes that tend to bulge, especially when she's vexed. She's a busy woman, Aunt Edna, running the house, working the garden, putting up her prize-winning fruits and jellies, organizing church bazaars. And taking care of Gram.

Norma Jean did as she was told. She kept her questions to herself in the downstairs part of the house. But in the attic her need to know and her imagination ran free. Who *were* the Taylors, those ancestors that made up her family—where did they come from? what were their lives like? where did they go? and most of all, what happened to her grandfather Travis and Julia, her young mother?

Uncle Frank seems so distant she doesn't even try to ask him anything. She knows her Grandpa hired him as a farm hand when he was still in his teens, and he and Aunt Edna ended up getting married. He's out in the fields most of the day and down at the barn till late. When he does come in, his nose is usually stuck in the local newspaper. When Norma Jean was little, she used to follow his lanky frame around the barnyard as he took care of the animals. He didn't talk much then either, but he answered all her questions about the cows, the chickens, the stray cats. He moved at a slow steady pace, talking to the animals, petting them as he passed out their feed. He showed her a litter of kittens in the corn crib and, when the mother was killed, taught her how to feed them.

Once, as she watched him milk the cow, she asked about her father. "Uncle Frank, it's like you're my daddy. But where is my *real* daddy?" He paused a second in his milking, and Bessie turned her big head to look at him.

"Well," he cleared his throat, "He wasn't from around here, a farm worker, passing through. We don't know where he is."

Norma Jean can't remember when she stopped tagging along with Uncle Frank—or why. When she was around twelve or thirteen, it just stopped happening. She got busy with other things, Aunt Edna needed her more in the house—and it began to seem a bit awkward. Yet she has a feeling that, if he *would* talk to her, he'd understand her questions.

Poor Gram never recovered from her stroke. She hasn't spoken for years; Norma Jean's never heard her say a word. Long ago they'd moved her bed downstairs to the parlor, the warmest room in the house and next to the kitchen. Most of the parlor furniture was moved across the hall and combined with the dining room which was closed off in winter to save heat.

Each morning she's not in school, Norma Jean bathes and dresses Gram; and Uncle Frank or Aunt Edna put her in the comfortable armchair by the fireplace. Nowadays she spends most of the day just looking out the window or staring into the fire, as though nothing were there at all. Norma Jean has to work hard to get her attention, taking a limp hand in both of hers, or getting right in front of her face and cupping each cheek like you would with a child.

"No one can reach her like you do, Norma Jean," says Aunt Edna looking in from the doorway to the kitchen. "You never knew Mama before her stroke, but you two are a lot alike, on the quiet side and thoughtful. Me, I don't have that kind of patience."

Yet, silent as Gram is, she's the one who taught Norma Jean to quilt when she was just a child. The old woman's fingers were more nimble then and nervous for work. She couldn't put whole quilts together anymore, but she could make the pieces, the squares and hexagons and pie-shaped triangles. The church women brought her the fabric, and she'd work for hours, sewing up one after another, concentrating as though her life depended on it. Norma Jean sat on a stool by her chair, trying to copy the motions; it came naturally to her and Gram would nod, almost smile when she got it right. Eventually, some of her own pieces went into the box of finished work that the quilters collected each month to put together.

But it's not just *Gram's* silence that makes the house quiet. There is little talk here anyway. Aunt Edna speaks mainly to give out directions or information. "Clean out the refrigerator, Norma Jean." "Wash your hands." "Go call Frank in to supper." "Now watch how I fold these sheets. It's important you learn to do things right the first time. Then you won't waste time doing them over."

Sometimes it seems like they're four people living under one roof, but each in his or her own little world—they just happen to be in the same house, like the planets up in the solar system.

All the same, Norma Jean doesn't mind the quietness that much. She's used to it, and she likes to daydream, let her mind wander without intrusion. Since no one would answer her questions, she often made up answers for herself. The attic, removed from the busyness of farm and household, has been her *imagining* place. Aunt Edna seldom goes up there, has always seemed content for Norma Jean to use it as a playroom, out from under foot. Mrs. Miller, Shirleen's mother, would come to help out with Gram during the busy time of summer harvest and bring Shirleen with her. The two girls would spend all morning up there moving boxes around to make little rooms, pulling out old dolls and dressing them up for "tea parties." Norma Jean read them imaginary letters from "cousins" in far off places, and they both play-acted stories about aunts and uncles who came to visit. Amongst the clutter and disorder, Norma Jean could pretend to be part of a larger family that was different, warmer, more lively.

As she grew older, she went there to read or sketch or sew. Only one light bulb hangs from the ceiling, but the dusty windows on either end of the slant roof let in light. In winter it's cold, she has to dress

11

warmly and use an old blanket; but in summer she can clear out the musty air by opening the windows to catch the morning breeze.

Sometimes life in the attic seems more real to her than life in the floors below. She thinks of her mother's photograph and tries to picture how she dressed, moved about, the sound of her voice. She wonders what her father looked like, and what Gram would tell her if she could talk.

***

Norma Jean waits to board the school bus at the end of the lane. She's glad they live close enough to town that she's one of the last to get on board. By the time it reaches her, the bus is full of farm kids who've been picked up all over their side of the county. They take the familiar route down Black River Road, across the noisy wooden bridge, past the cotton gin and down the main street of Pine Grove, a typical small community in the middle of a large rural area. The necessary stores—Logan's General, Johnson's Market, Fisher's Insurance, Bob's Barbershop, etc.—run down both sides of Main Street. Where it intersects with Maple, an anonymous Confederate soldier stands on a pedestal, so gray and weathered that the names of those long-ago casualties have sunk into the stone. Behind the stores on each side a handful of residential streets run parallel. The three churches sit on various street corners. The old brick high school is on a rise at the far end of town.

At the other end, closer to the river, a neighborhood of colored families live clustered around their AME chapel. Those kids are bused out to the Negro School more central to the farming part of the county where most colored families live.

Norma Jean keeps her seat in the school bus until it has emptied, then makes her way down the aisle and steps off. She likes to avoid the loud talk and jostle of the other kids—boys punching each other, calling out silly things and showing off, girls in clusters, flirting and giggling.

She doesn't linger in the hallway, which feels suffocating in spring and early fall and freezing in the winter, talking and waiting for the bell like most of the others, but goes straight to her homeroom, edging along the wall, head ducked, and hoping to get there quickly and unnoticed. Her homeroom desk is next to Shirleen's who lives in town and comes in at the last minute each day, eager to relate all the gossip she's picked up in the hall. Shirleen always has a desperate crush on *some*body, and Norma Jean has to laugh as she reports every detail of what he's wearing, how his hair's combed, who he's talking to, and any glance she thinks he's sent her way.

Shirleen studies boys the way Norma Jean studies her schoolwork. They are long-time friends, but so different. They even *look* different. Shirleen, who was squat and pudgy as a child, developed her full teen-age figure early. Her thick black hair is usually pulled up in a pony-tail that bops around as she bounces down the hall. Norma Jean is taller, thinner (she calls herself "skinny") and angular. She wonders if she will ever "fill out." *Her* favorite subject is history. They have a new teacher this year, Mr. Davis, who is young and enthusiastic—you can tell he finds history exciting. And he has them do such different assignments than her previous history teachers, like outside reading that makes an era seem more real: a poem by Anne Bradstreet when they studied the Puritans, an essay describing the appearance and demeanor of Lee and Grant when they met at Appomattox, a story by Willa Cather when they were studying the western migration. Family sagas have always intrigued her; she's sure some of the Taylors headed west.

Last fall she got excited when Mr. Davis gave a Family History assignment, encouraging each student to look up names and dates in the family Bible, visit the family plot in the cemetery, ask questions of older family members to find out what their ancestors' lives were like. Norma Jean hoped she'd learn more about the Taylors, but Aunt Edna had little to contribute.

"What kind of learning is that?" she asked. "In my day we studied more important things like wars, and dates and significant events. What's the sense of getting bogged down in a family's everyday life a hundred years ago?"

13

She said the family Bible had gone with Travis' older sister to Ohio when she got married. She and her husband had both died in the influenza epidemic around 1918, and Aunt Edna has no idea what happened to the Bible.

At the old cemetery, Norma Jean wrote down some names and dates she found there: William and Annabelle Taylor who, according to the dates, could be Travis' parents; Willie and Mattie Lawrence Taylor, but the stone sunk too far in the ground to read the dates at all; a Maggie Taylor Burdell, and numerous small graves for babies and children whose names were too worn to read. Arthur Taylor, a great uncle whose funeral Norma Jean vaguely remembered attending, was buried on one side of Travis' grave; on the other side was a space for Gram, her name already chiseled into the stone. Next she saw her mother's small, plain headstone, **Julia Taylor 1916–1936**. But Aunt Edna was no help in filling in the lives of these relatives or even connecting their relationship.

Mr. Davis accepted her slim paper with understanding when she told him that was all she could find out. "Well, Norma Jean," he said, his blue eyes looking right at hers, "you're a good student, I'm sure you did the best you could. Just keep in mind that we're making history right now with our own lives. You might want to keep a journal of the things you do and think about, so there'll be a record for your future generations."

Norma Jean thought that was an interesting idea, a record for the future, though she hasn't gotten around to it. Her life right now feels more like treading water than making history. What has stayed with her is Mr. Davis looking at her with his clear blue eyes, and how strange those last words—"your future generations"—made her feel.

***

One thing Norma Jean loves about quilting is the design, laying it out. Even though you've drawn out a plan, you never know how it's going to look until the pieces are in place. Moving them around, stepping back and looking, moving them around again—all this shuffling and looking and deciding excites her. It makes all the

14

difference, she thinks, in whether you end up with an ordinary quilt or something special, something people take real pleasure in seeing.

One rainy day she's up in the attic looking through an old chest for quilt material, old dresses or blouses that can find new life as part of a quilt. She woke up that morning with the idea of a *family* quilt, a kind of quilt album in place of the picture album that doesn't seem to exist. She thought of the trunks of old clothes up there, everything from baby clothes to mourning clothes, all hand-made. She'd looked through them when she was younger, being careful to put things back just as they were found, though she doubted anyone but herself ever saw them. Now her excitement about this new project makes her bold. She's the only one who cares about these old things anyway. She can use them as she likes. Aunt Edna probably won't mind; she's big on making use of everything, wasting nothing. It's odd that she hasn't cleaned out the attic, given everything away long before now. Maybe that's too much *past* for her to deal with. On the rare occasions she's wanted something from there, she's sent Norma Jean up to get it.

This new feeling of assertion gives her energy. She goes through the trunks in a different way, laying aside items that appeal to her. If this is to be a family quilt, everyone possible must be represented, either by their clothing or their handiwork. Though she doesn't know their names, she gets an idea of the different individuals by holding up shirts and dresses and comparing the sizes. Style is a clue to time period. So are groupings. One chest contains a Civil War uniform near the bottom, and she can see a timeline of clothing running from the floor of the trunk to the top.

She also sees individual differences in the stitches on dresses, aprons, and tablecloths, all fine quality work. How odd it seems to be holding up, shaking out, smoothing down clothes that members of her own family have worn, gotten up in the morning and dressed themselves in, washed and ironed and hung in their cupboards. Handling these outfits, holding them in her arms, makes these shadowy relatives more real to her, as though with a slight shift in time they could all be living here together. The quality of the work, the even stitches and careful tailoring inspires her, too. She has come from a family of seamstresses.

15

The album quilt will be a mosaic of as many members of her family as she can assemble. She likes thinking of the whole stream of them living in the house, working the land, making these clothes. The quilt pieces will tell the story. The thin stripes of men's shirts. The printed muslin and dimity of summer dresses, bright or subdued as reflects each personality. The wools and gabardines of winter. She imagines a Confederate soldier going off to war in the uniform, a young wife, dressed in a long yellow-flowered print, standing on the porch with two children, all waving until he's out of sight. A white linen tablecloth could have been a trousseau item, laid out for Sundays and holidays. A blue checked pinafore she sees on a young girl of ten or eleven, skipping rope, her braids flying up with each bounce. She works slowly in selecting these pieces, smoothing each fabric, tracing the patterns with her finger.

Norma Jean is in the midst of laying out the garments from the third chest when she discovers the false bottom. Underneath, covered with tissue paper, lies a quilt square she has never seen.

The colors of this square, even in the bottom of the dark chest, strike her heart, and several minutes pass before she reaches down to touch it, gingerly, as though the fabric might turn to dust before her eyes. Emerald green, royal blue, gold and vermilion—rich, passionate splashes of color like jewels ray outward from a central point, a circle of interspersed triangles, velvets and satins, the fabric of tapestries and draperies, of ball gowns of another day, all unpatterned, save for a border of renaissance roses in shades of pink and peach.

Carefully, fearing she is disturbing, violating even, some sacred place, she lifts the piece out of the trunk, an eight-inch square, it seems, but as finished and beautiful as though it covers the whole universe. As she holds it up to the weak streams of light coming through the dusty windows, the colors glow and ripple across the surface with the least movement.

She's never seen or heard of such a miniature quilt. She holds it against her breast, feeling privy to a carefully hidden treasure, one she wants to explore, but not betray. Julia's, she thinks. It must be hers.

16

She's been here in the attic, also, waiting for me to find her, as clearly as the photograph in the barn.

***

Shirleen passes a note to Norma Jean in English class: *Movies Friday night?*

She frowns. She loves movies, has seen *Gone with the Wind* five times, but the closest theater's in Jackson twenty miles away.

"How can we do that?" she asks when they're out in the hall.

"I think I can get Daddy to take us in, and maybe we'll get a ride home."

"With who?"

"Oh, I don't know, someone from out this way. I heard John Tom and Bobby Newman talking about going. It's a good movie I think."

"Shirleen! I know you have a crush on John Tom, but I am not riding with Bobby Newman—even in his dad's red Studebaker."

"Why? You'd be in the front seat and he'd be driving. He's not so bad, just, well, not terrific looking—and a little silly."

"And immature and stupid and drooly. Besides, he already asked me, and I told him no."

"He asked you already? Norma Jean! If you'd said O.K., John Tom might have asked me, and we'd have a double date. Dang! Don't you ever think of anyone but yourself?"

"I'm sorry, Shirleen. I just don't like him; he gives me the creeps."

"What excuse did you give him?"

"Just said I couldn't go. I'm hoping he won't ask again."

"*Why* are you so stand-offish? Don't you *like* boys? If you don't watch out, Norma Jean, you're going to end up an old maid living on the farm with Miss Edna." Shirleen sighs. "They're so strict with me at

17

home, you'd think they'd never been young themselves. But they think highly of you, Norma Jean. They'll usually let me do things if you're along."

"Don't be mad, Shirleen. We'll think of something else to do. There's Friday night square dancing in the school gym. If I come to your house straight from school, we could cut out that new skirt you want, and I'll stitch it up for you."

Shirleen frowns, considering. "All right, I guess it's better than nothing. Do you think you could stitch it in time for me to wear it that night?"

***

Norma Jean hasn't been square dancing all that long, but she's surprised how much she likes it—learning the calls and dancing them to the music. On Friday afternoon she shows Shirleen a few of the basic steps, and they're soon heel and toeing in their sock feet around the living room, stepping on each other's toes and giggling till Mrs. Miller, worried about her knickknacks, shoos them out to the front porch. Norma Jean smiles to herself; she's noticed before how dainty and precise everything is in the Miller household—so different from their farmhouse where things are kept wherever they'll best be at hand the next time they're needed.

"Mothers!" says Shirleen plopping down on the glider. "She's such a pill sometimes. 'Do this, don't do that.' It drives me crazy. You're a good teacher, Norma Jean, but I'll probably step on everyone's feet."

Mrs. Miller opens the front door, emitting the strong aroma of corned beef and cabbage.

"You girls come on in to dinner," she calls. "You don't want to be jumping around too soon after you eat. If Dad's not too tired, we might come over to take a look."

"Oh, Mama," Shirleen says quickly, "it'll be too noisy; you won't like it."

"Maybe, but we'll just watch a while, see who you girls are dancing with."

Norma Jean doesn't have to look to know that Shirleen is rolling her eyes.

***

Norma Jean sets her box of fabric scraps on the table and struggles out of her jacket. An early June storm is brewing outside, winds picking up and clouds hanging black and heavy in the sky; it's cooler than usual too, but to Norma Jean the wildness feels invigorating. "I'm doing pieces for a new quilt I've started at home," she says.

"What kind of quilt?" asks Bea Jones. "Let's see what you've got."

Norma Jean smiles, but shakes her head. "Not yet. It's a family quilt. But the design's not worked out yet. I've been pulling pieces out one at a time, letting them speak to me. It's slow this way, but I've got to work with it a while on my own."

"Well," says Bea, "I been quilting a long time, and I must say I never heard a piece of material *speak*. You won't end up with much if you don't plan it out. You know, there's people in this room with lots more experience than you."

"Your family's always been quilters," says Miss Ella Mae, "all except Edna." She laughs. "She's too busy *doing* to sit and make quilts. It'll be real interesting to see what you do with this, Norma Jean."

"Think on the center, child. Once you know the center, the rest will come along all right." Ethel smiles as if she already sees it and approves.

Norma Jean smiles also. She knows what the center will be, but it's the last thing she wants anyone to see. She needs to hold Julia's secret close for a while. Reaching into her box, she pulls out a piece of the material with the beautiful roses. Suddenly, she's aware that the others have stopped sewing and are looking her way.

19

"Where did you get this fabric, child?" Miss Ella Mae's kind eyes seem to be looking into her soul.

"I found it—up in the attic—in the bottom of an old trunk." Norma Jean feels herself coloring as she stutters out her reply.

"Has Edna seen it?"

"Noooo. I don't want them to see any of the pieces till the quilt's finished. This piece, it's beautiful—but you all look so strange. What is there about it—something I don't know?"

"I think," says Ethel, "you should show it to Edna."

***

Norma Jean is flustered and frustrated. She wants to ask the questions, not be asked them. And she never likes being the center of attention. As soon as she gets home, she calls up Shirleen and asks if they can walk to her house tomorrow after school.

"Shirleen, I know you've said your mother never mentions Julia, but won't you try again to find out *something*? You know, like if I look like her, or am I about the same size—just something casual."

"Well, I could try, but, you know, Norma Jean, I'm not very good at being subtle. I tend to just blurt things out."

"You see, Aunt Edna won't talk to me about anything up in the attic. The past is past she says, no good to dwell on it. But isn't it *my* past, too? My family's past, even though I wasn't born yet? We don't even keep a picture of my mother, but they all knew her."

Later Shirleen reports no success. "You know how my mother is, so vague. Sometimes I wonder where her mind is—or if something's wrong with her hearing. When I asked who she thought you looked like, she just stared at the soup she was stirring and said, "Hmm, well, that's always hard to say."

At the next quilting session, Norma Jean kept her eyes on the quilt they were stitching and said, "There's lots of quilts in our house,

20

but I don't know who made them. Miss Ella Mae, was my mother a quilter?"

For a few minutes no one speaks. She looks at the circle of women watching her; their silence feels thick as a stone wall. Finally, Ella Mae puts down her work. "Well, if your Grandma could talk, poor soul. . . . Your mother could make quilt pieces as young as you did, Norma Jean. She could have made anything. She was that good with a needle."

"Not that she had much to show for it," Bea mutters.

"Well, Julia didn't make things for show. She wasn't that kind of a steady worker. No, she made things she could throw herself into. She made clothes for herself, but she had to *love* the material. She made beautiful aprons for your Grandma when she was young, just twelve or so. Once she made the prettiest handkerchief for me, all hemstitched around the edges and little forget-me-nots embroidered in the corners— a Christmas present when I was her Sunday school teacher. I'll show it to you sometime."

Norma Jean looks down at the fabric on her lap. "She wore a dress made of these roses, didn't she? You all saw her in it. And it was special."

An immense stillness fills the room.

"Well," Miss Ella Mae says, turning back to her quilting, "your mother wore a lot of pretty dresses. Now, Ethel, what do you think about this yellow piece next to the lavender?"

CHAPTER 2

Norma Jean sits on the front porch shelling peas. She splits the hulls open unconsciously, emptying the small white lady peas into a glass bowl and dropping the husks onto the old newspaper spread out in her lap. Uncle Frank sits close by reading today's paper, but she is thinking about the way the quilting women clammed up on her last night as though she'd asked some shameful questions. It's like there's a conspiracy around to keep her from knowing about her mother, and the more she runs into it, the more she wants to find out.

"Says here President Eisenhower's expecting a truce with Korea this summer. Lots of young men will be glad to read that. And listen to this," Uncle Frank reads, turning the page: *"The latest census indicates around 240,000 farmers gave up farming in the last two years,"* Norma Jean feels her frustration rising. She can't understand Uncle Frank's absorption in the daily news which he reads faithfully after their noon dinner. It seems to her that by the time you read one day's news, the paper is already being laid out to print for the next day, the new pages only slight variations on the same reports. Right now he sits in a porch rocker next to her, the full paper opened out in front of him. She watches the peas build up in her bowl while she builds up the courage to interrupt him.

"Uncle Frank," she begins in a voice so soft she might be talking to the peas, "how old was my mother when you and Aunt Edna married?"

The rocking stops for a second or two and then begins again as her uncle clears his throat. "Can't say for sure," he mutters and turns to a new page, straightening out the flimsy newsprint with a pull on the edges that makes it crackle.

"Well, I guess you were on the farm long enough to know her pretty well, weren't you? When she was in her teens, I mean."

"Norma Jean, I'm trying to read the paper," Uncle Frank says without lowering his shield. "Why don't you go inside and sit with your grandma while you do that shelling?"

She looks out past the barn toward the fields where the young corn stalks are shining bright green in the early summer sun. Beyond that, one of last year's bean fields lies brown and fallow, waiting for a fall planting. To the far side, a line of trees and brambles marks the banks of the Black River. Everything starts blurring together through the tears that are filling her eyes. She realizes she has quit her pea-shelling, but she doesn't stir.

22

"I want to know what she was like, that's all, what kind of person she was." Her mind's eye gazes at the photograph in the barn. "Who do you think she looked like? Did she look at all like me?" She can hear the catch in her voice and feels her face reddening.

Uncle Frank slowly lowers his paper, looks at her, and then looks away, out over the same fields and off into the distance.

"Norma Jean," he says and his voice sounds tired, "I know Edna has never spoken to you much about Ju—about your mother. And now there are things you want to know. That's natural, I guess, only natural. But it's hard to talk about her. And sometimes there are things we're better off *not* knowing. Far better off, believe me." She hears a heaviness in his voice that she's never heard before.

"Edna has her reasons, good reasons. And Gram is fragile; we don't want to stir up memories. She's had about all she can take. Maybe you should go on with your own life, let these questions rest."

Norma Jean is moved by his kindness and the weariness of his expression; his warning echoes her own uneasiness. But she feels compelled to go on.

"Just tell me a little bit about her," she says. "She seems so mysterious; what was she like? Uncle Frank, please tell me *some*thing."

He slowly folds the paper together, then in half, smoothing the crease with his thumb and forefinger. Sighing a deep sigh, he reaches in his shirt pocket for the bag of tobacco he always has there and, with a thin paper from his other pocket, slowly rolls a cigarette, strikes a match to light it, and blows out a stream of smoke.

"Julia," he begins, looking off across the fields, "was a person unto herself. Unusual that is, surely different for these parts. And as different from her sister, from Edna, as you can imagine. It's hard to pin it down though, to explain just how she was. Where Edna is practical, Julia was—well, I don't think she even understood that word. And where Edna is serious about getting things done, Julia was . . . playful, I guess you could call it, chasing butterflies, climbing trees. Sometimes walking dreamlike through the yard, smiling to herself like she had a big secret."

For a moment he seems lost in reverie, and Norma Jean is surprised to see the softness that has settled over his face. He stirs in his chair as if about to rise.

"Aunt Edna was almost ten years older, wasn't she?"

"Well, yes. She had a hand in raising her, too. But it was a great exasperation to her, Julia's ways. She thought Travis and Gram had spoiled her rotten." He gives a short laugh and looks down at his hands, now clasped and resting on the folded paper.

"You know the work it takes to run this farm, Norma Jean. Another article in the paper here today about the 'plight of post-war farming': crops no longer needed, land values down, young folks moving to the cities for more pay, easier work. I don't know what Travis would make of all that!"

"I guess it's easier for farmers if they raise a crop of boys," Norma Jean says. "Did people think Julia was just lazy?"

"There were those that called her lazy—other things too: self-centered, willful, even simple. I can't say I agreed with any of those things, except maybe the willfulness. Though she come by that naturally enough, I guess. Your granddaddy Travis was about as willful as they come. Had his own ideas about how things ought to go, on the farm and elsewhere. And there weren't much arguing with him. Often enough, he was right, too."

"Did he get along with them, with Aunt Edna and Julia?"

"Get along? Well, he was the one in charge for sure. Edna's a lot like him. He taught her everything about running the farm, and she picked it up easy. I think he was very satisfied with her. But Julia . . . Julia was his treasure, his little darling. She softened his edges. Yet she could be as stubborn as he was. Well, maybe stubborn's not the right word, *or* willful. She just followed her heart, that's all, and didn't heed anything else."

24

Uncle Frank stops speaking and for a few minutes Norma Jean remains quiet. She's trying to see the young girl in the photo laughing, singing, playing around the farm. The picture he paints sounds so different from their quiet and serious life on the farm now. She looks up at Uncle Frank with another question in her eyes. But he's already rising, sticking the paper under his arm. The conversation has ended.

"That's all I can tell you, Norma Jean. Anything else you want to know, you'll have to ask Edna."

***

July comes in hot and dry. Shirleen and her family are planning a trip out to Ohio to visit relatives, and they invite Norma Jean to come along. But Aunt Edna says she's needed at home. Summer's a busy time on the farm. Shirleen's not looking forward to the long car trip with only her parents, but she perks up when she learns that one of her cousins, a little squirt when she last saw him, is now captain of his high school football team.

Norma Jean's just as happy to stay in Pine Grove. There's not much spare time to work on her quilt, and the attic's stifling in the afternoon anyway. But she carries it around in her head, and early mornings, whenever she gets a chance, she spreads out her fabrics and sketches possible designs. Once she took them to the hayloft and propped up Julia's photograph for inspiration. It gave her a sense they were doing something together. Somehow working on this quilt gives her the feeling she's piecing together the family picture, getting a little closer to understanding her history, though it would be hard to explain, even to herself, why this is so. At least she's doing *something*.

Otherwise her mind has been occupied by thoughts of the Black River. This place where her nineteen-year-old mother drowned has always haunted her. Though it runs just beyond their far property line, she's glad it's bordered by trees and thick growth and can't be seen from the downstairs part of the house. But in the attic, the angle is different. There are two places where gaps in the trees and the early morning light reveal the water moving along, and lately it's been calling to her, *Black River, Black River*—the words recurring again and again like a shadowy

25

theme on the edge of her mind. Even in the attic as she arranges and rearranges strips of material, she cannot escape her awareness of it. Somehow she knows that exploring its banks, observing its flow, is the next step she must take to uncover the mystery.

***

Norma Jean stoops to pull a thorn loose from her jeans and looks around carefully for her next step. The edges of the fields along the river are so chock full of weeds, brambles and hawthorns, wild raspberries and greenbriars, it's hard to move without being caught or scratched. It seems all the wild growth that used to live in the fields has been pushed to the river, guarding it against trespass.

She wonders if this thorny barrier has any relation to the Black River's name, though she's been told it's because of the oaks and evergreens growing along its banks, darkening the river with tannin. There's nothing rippling or babbling about these shadowy waters moving steadily, stealthily, unobserved in these parts except from the narrow bridge crossing over on the county road upstream. And the times it floods its banks and submerges the fields after heavy spring rains.

Although the Black River runs beside their farm, Norma Jean does not really know it at all. She hasn't wanted to know more about it, the river that ended her mother's life. The name alone chills her senses as though any water connected to drowning can only be sinister, something to avoid. So what strange force is leading her to pick her way through this thicket, holding a long, looping stem of thorns down with her foot only to be surprised by another?

When she finally works her way through to the bank, she's disappointed to find the growth in both directions too thick for her to move along the water's edge. The other side looks more passable, but the river is wide here, twenty feet or more with no way to cross. Holding on to a small tree trunk and leaning out over the bank, she can see the water narrows a bit upstream where a fallen tree lies across its width. She backtracks a few feet, stoops under a tangle of vines and branches, and with care and vigilance makes her way forward. She's getting better

26

at finding the best passage, seeing the hazards around her, and circling when she can't go through.

Hot and sweaty, she finally reaches the log and stops to wipe her face and look around. There's a bend in the river just beyond the fallen tree where the water slows and spreads out in a way that looks cool and inviting. And she can hear the soft flow of the water—not rippling or gurgling, but steady, more like a faucet left running in another room. The trees overhead and the heavy brush screen the area from the world, giving it the feeling of a woodsy cave. In this wild place, Norma Jean recognizes a familiar feeling, the safety and privacy of her place in the attic.

She climbs up on the log, holding the trunk firmly with both hands, and crawls slowly out over the river. The moss feels soft and squishy after the rough brambles, but doesn't offer a firm grip. Whenever she can, her hands grasp the old rough bark while her knees seek the mossy cushion. The tree seems stable enough, but it's been there a long time. She doesn't completely trust it.

Midway across she looks down into the dark running water beneath. A strange feeling sweeps through her, a sense of the world moving, spinning, passing on forever into infinity. And herself, a tiny fixed point in the universe, clinging to an ancient tree over a timeless river, yet part of the whole scene.

Reaching the far bank, she drops down and makes her way towards the river's bend. Her feet sink into the silt and sand that have built up here over time, forming a beach-like flat. Behind it the steeply rising bank is a jumble of honeysuckle and wild primrose. She stands perfectly still looking at the roses, hearing the river, and breathing in the sweet fragrance. Somehow she knows this place. She has been here before, perhaps in a dream. She sinks to her knees as the recognition becomes clear.

Of course. This was *Julia's* place. She feels it in some unexplainable way. A secret place where her mother came, a place very special to her. A wave of pure joy washes through Norma Jean's body. Picking up a nearby stick, she writes bold letters in the silt: JULIA'S

***

August seems like the busiest month of the year with corn ripening in the fields, tomatoes heavy on the vines and peaches ready to be picked off the tree. Aunt Edna is busy from dawn till evening parboiling, peeling, slicing, and filling the canning jars with farm food they will eat throughout the winter.

Today they are putting up peaches, and Norma Jean, sitting at the old oak table writing out labels for the jars, is aware of her aunt's sure movements around the kitchen, how she never seems hurried or harried, cross or unhappy. On the other hand, she is seldom excited or serene. Just focused on her task, thinks Norma Jean, her fruit and knives, pans and jars laid out in order around the sink and stove. No steps will be wasted. A full-sized apron covers her yellow checked house dress, and the square fat heels on her sturdy black shoes make business-like taps as she walks across the linoleum.

Like generations of Taylor women before her, Aunt Edna reaches into the bushel basket of soft, fuzzy fruit, inspects for bruises and flaws, plops them into boiling water to soften the skin, then inserts the knife to release the sweet-sharp fragrance of ripe peaches. Hanging on a string by the basement stairs, is a brown spiral notebook filled with canning records from years past, the quarts of beans, beets, strawberries, peaches put up each year, a mark checking off each one as it's used. Norma Jean has never paid much attention to it, but she's seen Aunt Edna carefully entering the figures for each canning session, then totaling up the season's list. She's also noticed when the handwriting changes from what must have been Gram's delicately slanted script to the bold blockish print of Aunt Edna.

She wonders if her mother ever sat where she is sitting writing labels or doing some other task. She can see her with Gram, but, from the sparse information she has, it's hard to imagine her working side by side with Aunt Edna. Still, thinks Norma Jean, Julia would love the peach trees in bloom and the smell of fresh cut peaches just as I do.

Norma Jean sighs and stacks the labels in piles (Alberta, Freestone, Redskin, 1953) to be ready when the jars, their lids tightly sealed, come off the stove, the bright fruit of one season carefully preserved for seasons to come. Using her long-handled colander, Aunt Edna scoops up a new batch of peaches from the boiling water, dumps them into the round enameled dishpan and sets them on the table. She sits down across from Norma Jean, picks up her paring knife, and begins to efficiently peel away the skin.

It's unusual to be sitting with Aunt Edna, working together at the kitchen table, almost like the cozy, mutual feeling of the quilting circle. This might be a good time to get her to talk. But before she can speak, her aunt's voice interrupts her train of thought.

"Norma Jean, you're sixteen—seventeen next February—and about to start your senior year. It's time we started making plans for your future. Have you thought about that?"

"Oh!" says Norma Jean, startled and wary of the question, "Well, not specifically." She knows Aunt Edna likes to get things settled, would probably like to wrap up the whole question right here in the kitchen this morning. But Norma Jean is far too preoccupied with figuring out her past right now to make decisions about the days to come.

"Well, I have," says Edna, giving her a serious look across the table. "There's not much use you thinking about working full time here at the farm; you just don't have the stamina for it, and, frankly, you don't have the temperament either. Though I do appreciate your willingness. . . ."

She pauses a moment, a large peach in one hand, the knife held up in the other. "Yes, willingness to be responsible, to do your part, can carry you far. And, where it's missing," she nods her head decisively, "you find a flawed character. It's been a big relief you haven't turned out like . . . like that." Aunt Edna purses her lips and sighs a deep sigh. "But willingness aside, the truth is, it often takes longer to show you how to do something than to do it myself."

Aunt Edna rises to parboil another batch of peaches. As she stands at the stove with her broad back turned to the table, her flour sack apron tied neatly in place, she seems to typify a farm woman, strong and plodding as a workhorse in the fields, enduring all kinds of hardships, prevailing in her steadiness. Norma Jean feels a flicker of sympathy for her large ungainly aunt, so plain in appearance, so lacking in grace. Aunt Edna brings over a new batch of steaming peaches and reaches for her knife.

"Course you can *live* here long as you want, helping out as best you can. And we've always intended you'd get a share of the farm's income when you're grown. But the way farming's going these days, I don't think you can count on that for support . . . that is, unless you *marry* a farmer. And I can't see that happening either. Not that many young men going into farming these days."

Norma Jean thinks of Uncle Frank, how he had come to the Taylor farm as a hired hand, happy to be taken on, his own father a tenant farmer having no land to give him. How content he seemed to be farming and working the land. Aunt Edna's right, it's very different today.

But she feels tense. It isn't that often Aunt Edna *speaks* what she's thinking. Her *looks* say plenty, thick eyebrows squinched together over her bulging eyes, mouth pressed downward. She goes about her own business, not inclined to conversation. But when she does speak out, it's like she's been mulling the matter over for days and has come to some clear and unshakeable conclusion. Now she's planning Norma Jean's *life*.

She feels a surge of panic and queasiness like the time at the county fair when she was persuaded by Shirleen to ride the tilt-a-whirl. She knew the minute they snapped down the safety bar that she should get off. But the roll had already started, there was no way out, nothing to be done but wait for it to end.

Aunt Edna keeps her eyes on her work, cutting a perfect curl of peach skin that drops onto the growing pile she will toss to the hogs.

"I was talking to Ethel Posey the other day down at the store. She thinks you're right smart with a needle, especially for your age. But

I never heard of anybody supporting themselves making quilts. Takes too long and most people around here have quilts in their family anyway."

She dumps the scraps in the slop bucket. Selecting a peeled peach, she cuts a quick circle around, pulls it apart, and pushes out the rough seed with her thumb revealing its bristly red interior.

"It's possible you could go to Jackson and train with someone there, then set up shop as a seamstress if there's enough demand for them. Or you might find work at a dry goods store in Jackson, full time instead of just Saturdays at Logan's."

As she talks her hands slice the peach into quick even sections. "Then there's teaching and nursing, reliable fields for young women, but they take training. We'd be hard pressed to find the money."

Norma Jean's head is spinning with all this talk. It seems like Aunt Edna is speaking of someone else, someone from a different time, a different place, like a character in a book or movie. She feels numb, speechless. But Aunt Edna, her knife inserted in a dripping peach, is looking straight at her and waiting for a response.

"I . . . I . . . Aunt Edna, I . . ." The words come out in a rush. "When I was born . . . sixteen years ago . . . what happened? Why did my mother drown? What happened to Grandpa? And who was my father? I *have* to know!"

The older woman's forehead wrinkles in consternation, and her eyes bug out like she's seeing something unnatural. They settle on Norma Jean, studying her intently. Norma Jean waits, her heart beating fast. She feels like she's standing at the mouth of a cave, one that tunnels into darkness, a vast cavern that, once entered, allows no turning back. Peach juice drips to the table from Aunt Edna's hands. When she speaks her voice is flat.

"Daddy," she pauses. "Daddy had a heart attack. Julia drowned, I don't *know* why. And I have no idea who your father is."

"But . . . but why do you *think* she drowned, who *might* my father have been? Was there a connection between Grandaddy's heart attack and all this?"

"I don't want to think about any of that, Norma Jean. I feel myself getting all agitated." She rises abruptly from the chair and stands facing the window, her large hand still holding the sticky knife and grasping the edge of the sink.

She's never seen Aunt Edna upset in this way. She hasn't meant to hurt her. A sudden clap of thunder makes them both jump. Aunt Edna grabs the laundry basket and heads for the clothesline as she calls out, "Watch the stove, Norma Jean. Don't let those peaches boil over! Just keep them at a simmer."

She returns with a basketful of damp clothes and a sigh of resignation. When she speaks, her voice is flat and weary. "Norma Jean, as I've told you, that was a trying time. The only way we were able to move on from it was to put it out of mind. Now you're wanting to bring it all up again." Norma Jean looks down at the table and waits.

"None of us *knows* what happened then. Too much happened too fast for any sense to be made of it." Aunt Edna's voice becomes stern, almost angry. "Julia was like that, secretive and impulsive, always set on having her own way. And you could never depend on her for anything around the farm. Only if she *felt* like it."

Norma Jean winces at the bitter edge in her aunt's voice.

"She fell for a drifter, far as we can tell. A feller who'd been doing part-time farm work in the area. No one knew about it when they were about to run off—just planning to disappear into thin air, I guess."

Aunt Edna stops her work and puts the knife on the table. She removes her glasses and rubs the place between her eyes where they've left pinch marks.

"Somebody, I don't know who, told Daddy." She seems to be reciting words she has gone through in her mind many times. "He took his shotgun and went after them. When time had passed and they didn't return, Frank and Joe Turner went looking. Found Daddy dead in the

32

field, heart attack the doctor said. The gun'd been shot, but why and how we don't know. Looked like there'd been some kind of a tussle. Julia was wandering about like she was in a trance or something. Turned out she was near five months pregnant, and none of us knew about that either! The drifter was nowhere to be seen."

The scene plays out in Norma Jean's mind like a movie. How awful it must have been—for all of them. And her mother right in the middle.

She thinks of her picture in the photograph. She thinks of the sandy beach where the river bends round, the hiddenness of it, the roses and honeysuckle. She had imagined a dark-haired young woman wearing a full-skirted dress of roses dancing lightly across the sand, her arms waving through the air like wheat stalks in the fields. And a young man watching her, a blue bandana tied loosely around his sun-tanned neck, smiling a carefree, open smile. How could it all have turned so ugly!

"What was his name?" Norma Jean asks in a voice that sounds small and far away even to herself.

"His *name*?" Aunt Edna gives her an incredulous look. "*I* don't know. Don't know and don't care. Do drifters have names? Probably a different one in every town. That was the last thing I was thinking on. The sheriff looked for him to find out what happened since Julia wouldn't say *anything*. No luck there. Of course, he never showed up on his own. Too scared, I guess. So much for true love!"

Norma Jean stares out the window feeling drained and defeated. No matter what she asks, or when or where, Aunt Edna is resistant, unwilling to go beyond the most basic details. The pain she feels for her young mother makes it difficult to speak. She feels tears rising to the surface. Aunt Edna starts to busy herself, clearing the table to make room for the Mason jars, already sterilized and ready to be filled. At the stove she checks the canning water, then arranges the jars in a circle around the big crock of sliced peaches.

"It's foolish to rake all this up. Upsetting to everybody. That chapter is over. What's done is done. Now, Norma Jean, what you need is to look ahead, think about the future, and plan what you want to do."

***

"I wonder," says Norma Jean without looking up from her needle, "just how many kinds of quilts there are." It's September, still daylight outside, and the quilters are in the back room of the church with the doors open, the rose aroma from the churchyard scenting the room. "I mean, before I thought much about it, it seemed the only kinds of quilts were the ones we have on our beds."

"Well, honey, there's all kinds of quilts, you know. The bed quilt is just the most traditional. Most likely how it all got started was people trying to stay warm by piecing together what little scraps they had to make a cover. Some who had a better eye than others got to making them more and more pretty and thought of other ways to use them."

"Other ways to make them, too," says Bea. "Some of the quilts in that quilting magazine at the Jackson library look like museum paintings. I don't think they should even call that a quilt—to my mind, a quilt ought to be useful."

"Something can be useful *and* pretty, can't it?" Miss Ella Mae asks. "You know, folks think wall quilts are something new, but back in the old days lots of folks hung quilts over windows in the winter to keep the drafts out. It can be right cheery having a big, colorful quilt on the wall."

"Those are big quilts," says Norma Jean, "but did you ever hear of a tiny quilt, even smaller than doll buggy size—just, you know, very finished, but tiny?" She holds up her hands to measure the size in the air.

Bea looks at her like she's crazy, but Ethel smiles and leans forward. "Oh," she says, "you must be talking about a *love pocket*. Lord, I haven't thought of those in ages!"

"A *love* pocket. For goodness sake—what kind of foolishness is that?" Bea never likes being told about anything *she* hasn't heard *first*.

"Well, Bea, that was way before *your* time, back when times were slower, back in the days of romance." Miss Ella Mae smiles, her eyes twinkling. "A young girl would make a quilt square—usually beautiful and in secret—that signified her feelings for someone special. She might even put his name in a little hidden pocket, or a love note she was too shy to give him. They were private little quilts though; people didn't show them around. The only one I ever saw was the one Mama found in Aunt Cora Whitley's cedar chest after she died. It was a great puzzle to the family because, far as anyone could remember, Aunt Cora never even had a beau."

***

"Doesn't it feel different being a senior?" asks Shirleen. "It felt so special the first day, knowing we were top dog, knowing it's my last year in a Pine Grove school. Those ninth graders look like babies."

Shirleen is wearing one of the new-style "poodle skirts." The complete circle of cloth with a white felt poodle appliquéd on one side swirls out like a ballerina's when she twirls around. She's trying to get her mother to let her perm her hair in the new poodle-cut style. They both wear their saddle shoes with white rolled-down socks.

"Yeah, it's different," Norma Jean agrees. "Kind of scary, too. We've never had to think about where we'll be in September, but next year, who knows?" Aunt Edna's prodding about her plans for the future has sharpened her own anxious feelings. "I'll be glad when Mr. Davis returns. His substitute just reads out paragraphs from the assignment we've already read, then has us write out answers to the questions at the end of the chapter. So boring."

"Norma Jean, haven't you heard? He's not coming back. He got a job teaching in a bigger school where his fiancée lives. The sub is just here till they find a regular teacher."

"His fiancée! Are you sure, Shirleen? Who told you? Maybe it's just a rumor."

"I'm sure. I heard the principal tell Miss Anderson. He sounded pretty mad that Mr. Davis had taken the other job at the last minute.

Norma Jean, you look so upset!" Shirleen widens her eyes. "Oh, my goodness. Were you sweet on *Mr. Davis*? And never *told* me."

"Don't be silly," Norma Jean answers, moving briskly down the hall. "He's just the best teacher I ever had, that's all."

***

The more Norma Jean thinks about graduation, about her future, the more she feels pulled into the well of her past. Why, she wonders, am I not looking ahead, making plans and dreaming dreams like everyone else? I'm not *afraid* to grow up; it doesn't feel like that at all. It's like sitting in a boat on a still lake, oars in place, but never dipping them into the water. She feels stuck, grounded, like she can't know what she wants, until she understands and explores her source, those springs and branches that came together to create *her* stream, the woods and valleys they went through, the debris gathered along the way.

She muses on these things as she moves through her days doing her housework and homework dutifully, but all the while listening, watching, waiting for what might come through. The only time her thoughts and actions are together is in the attic working with her fabrics. Here the questions and answers, though still illusive, are present in a calm way. When her fingers touch the cloth, when she looks at the colors and patterns of each one and smoothes it with her hand, she feels peaceful, a peace that holds a bright little spark.

She takes her time with this project, allowing it to slowly inform her. When the clothes have been cut up and the pieces laid out, the colors surrounding her look wonderful: blue and white striped cloth from a man's shirt; yards of black material sprinkled with tiny flowers from the long gathered skirt of a dress; a wide blue taffeta ribbon from a child's yellowed organdy pinafore; a rough twill weskit. She sits on the floor and arranges them around herself, a carousel of color, a family circle of texture and hue.

This quilt is hers alone to make, she the only one who can do it, who can take all these different materials and stitch them together into something whole. She spends as much time as possible with the fabrics, imagining each person who might have selected and worn them, envisioning the ones who made them. She moves the material around, creating different groupings in the circle and waiting for some kind of design, however tentative, to emerge.

Nothing comes for a long while, nothing that feels right. At some point she realizes she's trying to make them fit into patterns she already knows, ones she has used or seen before in the quilts of Pine Grove, patterns that are proven, rhythmic, even intricate, but set and predetermined. That won't work for her. She's doing a new kind of quilt, one personal to herself and her family. The design must be fresh and original.

This insight brings a new flow of energy. She cuts out small pieces of fabric to experiment with, tiny rectangles, triangles, circles, and squares. Her scissors create strips, snake-like curves, half-moons and diamonds. She absorbs herself in moving them about on the attic floor, arranging and rearranging, playing with the combinations. It's fun, more fun than she's ever had copying patterns from other quilts. The more she moves them around, the freer and more connected she feels. She knows she's on the right track.

To her surprise, unusual shapes emerge—not the neat, small squares she's accustomed to, but blocks of cloth, three, four, five inches in length that seem to fall into place. And pointed triangles, trapezoids, cloud-like shapes, zigzags. Also, long, thin strips that want to overlay the others in odd and irregular places. Taking up a pad, she tries to sketch out what's happening to get a sense of the whole design. That could be reassuring, but instead it feels flat and analytical. Am I going to have to do this whole thing piece by piece, she wonders, with no idea where I'm going? It's daunting, yet the possibility of working this way feels so alive, it outweighs her doubt.

She looks at the pieces around her, a cloth jigsaw puzzle with no picture to guide her. She imagines straight strips curving and looping and shooting off towards a corner. Her fingers move quickly, pushing the pieces about. She places one strip across another, but what if she only partially overlays it and leaves one end unattached, a few inches hanging loose and free? Or fringed? She's having such a good time with her tiny pieces, her miniature layout, she almost forgets the larger quilt it's intended to represent.

CHAPTER 3

"Don't you *want* to go to college?" asks Shirleen. "I mean, just to meet new people and hear about new things and all. Dottie Jones says there's lots of cute guys on campus."

"It costs too much money. Anyway, I don't think it's the right thing for me."

"But, Norma Jean, you're so smart. Miss Anderson says she knows you can get a scholarship. With a part-time job you could do it."

"Yeah, maybe, but I don't think so. It just doesn't feel like what I should do now. I don't know why, it just doesn't."

"Do you want to stay here *forever* in Pine Grove in that house full of old people

Shirleen looks so alarmed, so incredulous that Norma Jean has to smile. How can she explain to her friend what she doesn't understand herself?

"It's O.K., Shirleen. Don't worry about "forever." It's just that, for now, I need to stay here. You and I, we're different, that's all, but we're still friends; we'll always be good friends. Got to go now. See you."

Norma Jean walks off down Maple Street, glad to get away from Shirleen's anxious, insistent voice. Last week's wind and rain have brought an early fall. Crumpled leaves, sticks, dried stalks and grasses litter the walkway around her feet, and the October sky, overcast with doughy gray clouds, feels as fixed as a picture. A familiar feeling settles over her, a kind of floating stillness, drifting without moving, transparent and weightless. The houses on either side of the street seem unreal and distant, but the front porches feel like eyes watching her, seeing how she looks and walks, judging her mood, what she is thinking.

Suddenly she feels self-conscious. What if someone comes out of one of these doors? Speaking to anyone right now would be unbearable.

Pulling her coat close around her, she sets off down the street, no destination in mind, but at the edge of town, she breathes a sigh of relief. There on a little rise amidst ancient trees and shrubbery is the old cemetery, a timeless place where she can walk without intrusion, walk, and think, and listen.

This cemetery isn't used much anymore. Most burials now take place in the Memorial Gardens over towards Masontown where it's less expensive; without headstones the mowing and upkeep is easier.

Norma Jean wanders down the old paths, maintained just enough to get around on, and feels herself relaxing. How much more at ease she is here than at school or with friends or even in her own house, except for the attic. She won't tell Shirleen though, who thinks she's weird enough already. But she hopes she hasn't hurt her feelings. They are close friends. It's just that Shirleen is so open and talkative, always wanting to be around other people, to be a part of whatever's going on, while Norma Jean's much more private. It's only when she's alone, like now, that she can calm down and figure things out.

Yes, the cemetery's like the attic, peoples' lives all around her, waiting for her to notice but not pushing her this way or that, not asking her why she's different. Without thinking about it, she walks in the direction of her mother's grave. As she gets closer to the old cedar tree that marks the area, she slows down and is surprised to feel her heart beating rapidly, her breath growing short. It's not ghosts. She doesn't fear such things. No, it's more like anticipation, like walking on the edge of some huge space that could claim you or change you forever. The gravel crunching under her feet sounds too loud as she moves forward.

***

There it is, **Julia Taylor 1918–1936.**

It's hard to imagine the young girl of the photo buried here in the ground. Once in *LIFE* magazine she saw a picture of a cemetery in Italy where photographs of the deceased were attached to many of the grave markers. She'd thought it odd at the time, but now it seems a good idea. The Julia that *lived*, the mother that birthed her and held her, was much more present in her photograph, than in this pile of dirt. The tombstone has already started sinking into the ground, and a graying process has begun.

Norma Jean kneels down and steadies herself with a hand on the rough curved edge. With her right index finger, she traces the letters of her mother's name.

In the silence that surrounds her she feels their connection, more strongly than she has ever felt. Placing both hands on the center of the grave, she whispers, "I think I have found your heart. It's been waiting for me all these years, in the chest, in the attic. Thank you."

***

Norma Jean and Uncle Frank bounce along in the cab of the pickup trying to miss the worst of the ruts in the dirt lane leading up to their place from the county blacktop. November has been harsher than usual, already freezing, thawing, refreezing more than once; but there's no sense trying to fix it till after winter and the spring rains. Uncle Frank concentrates on steering, sometimes keeping the wheels in the low places, sometimes trying to ride the ridge on each side. He's good at it, Norma Jean thinks, careful and steady. But once the wheel slips down, and the bounce sends her up to the ceiling.

"You O.K.?" he says, his eyes still on the lane.

"Yeah," she answers, planting her feet firmly on the floor and grabbing the edge of the seat with both hands. Motion, fast or sudden, is not comfortable to her. Ever since the time Shirleen talked her into that awful ride on the Tilt-a-whirl at the county fair, she seldom ventures beyond the slow circular movement of the Ferris wheel.

"Maybe it's this doggone road that's kept you from wanting to drive. I could sure understand that. One of these years we'll get it graded down, put a new surface on."

Norma Jean smiles. She's heard this every year. But she has no interest in driving, even on a smooth road. Machinery feels unwieldy to

40

her. Motors are noisy and smelly and much too fast. She can't imagine herself trying to control all that power. She doesn't want to.

They are headed into Jackson, the county seat, a big town compared to Pine Grove which is really little more than a village. Uncle Frank has business to attend to, and Norma Jean has a list of things to get for Aunt Edna who is busy organizing the church's Christmas Bazaar. But the main thing on her mind is the library. She's been waiting for this opportunity ever since Bea Jones' remark a week ago when Norma Jean was waiting on her in Logan's.

Bea was buying denim that day to make coveralls for her boys. After gossiping with the Logan sisters and the other customers, she asked Norma Jean to measure off the right amount.

"Two and a quarter yards, Norma Jean. Not a bit more, you hear. I can hardly afford to dress these children nowadays, they're growing so fast."

Norma Jean kept her eyes on the long shears as she carefully cut across the grain.

"You know," said Bea lowering her voice and leaning over the counter, "you was asking us questions one night about your mother. People around here don't want to talk about that business, out of respect for your family, your grandma and grandpa and Edna. But you can read about it in *The County Bulletin*. They got all the back issues stored away in the library in Jackson. They'll pull them out for you, the ones you want."

Bea picked up her package and tucked it under her arm, then leaned in closer. "Don't bother trying to look up your birth announcement though. You won't find *that* in print."

It's funny I haven't done this earlier, Norma Jean thinks as they reach the outskirts of Jackson. I could have gone to the library, looked in the old papers. Why didn't I? She thinks of Aunt Edna's reluctance to talk about what happened and is aware of a fleeting hesitancy. How much does *she* want to know? And from a newspaper—so matter of fact

41

and public. Now it seems like Bea's words are challenging her to do it, calling her bluff in a way.

Norma Jean waits while the librarian goes into a backroom and looks through the papers. *The County Bulletin* comes out weekly and she's requested the four issues of March, 1936.

"Doing research?" asks the woman. "That's a good way to find out about the history of your home county. So many people know more about the rest of the world than the place where they live."

Norma Jean takes her papers to a far table. Her hands are trembling and she has to breathe deeply to steady herself. Slowly she turns through the first paper, March 4, 1936 The world of Burke County is laid out for her on the pages, the world her mother inhabited. She sees an article about street repair in Jackson, a picture of a 4H-er and his prize bull, an account of the fire that burned down the First Methodist Church. The same kinds of things one finds in the same paper today, only the hair styles look dated and the clothes are different—mid-calf skirts on the women, felt hats on the men; some of the ads are for places and products no longer available.

She turns through the pages, taking in the atmosphere of that time, imagining being a part of it. Of course, most of the pictures are of events in Jackson, but in a column called 'Farming Forecast,' she reads:

Local farmers say they have never seen so much water on their land. Most of the spring planting is drowned out. Black River has overrun its banks more times than anyone can count, and the rains are still coming down.

In the paper of March 25, 1936, she finds what she's looking for. On the front page she reads:

PINE GROVE WOMAN DROWNS IN BLACK RIVER

The body of Julia Taylor, a graduate of Pine Grove High School, was pulled from the floodwaters of the Black River Monday. She had been missing for two days when John McCall, a member of the search party, spied some clothing caught on a fallen branch in one of the more inaccessible parts of the river. It proved to be the skirt of the dress the

42

victim was wearing. Officers are investigating the details of the drowning. Anyone having information that might be helpful is asked to come forward. All citizens of Burke County are warned to stay clear of the river until the flooding subsides.

And in the Pine Grove section:

We regret the passing of Julia Taylor, a young woman known to everyone in Pine Grove. Her family has lived in these parts as long as anyone can remember. We extend our deepest sympathy to them at this sad time.

Then in the obituaries:

Julia Taylor, age 19, died March 20, 1936. She is survived by her mother, Agnes Taylor and her sister and brother-in-law, Edna and Frank Johnson.

No mention of an infant daughter.

***

Norma Jean says little on the way home and goes quickly to the attic. She's copied out the articles, but she doesn't need to read them again now. She'd hoped to find out more about the drowning, but the main thing that absorbs her is the fact, the reality of her mother's life. The newspaper reports of her death have given her that. Despite all the mystery that surrounds her and all of Norma Jean's daydreams, Julia Taylor was a real flesh and blood person. She lived here in this community, this house. There's no disputing her life.

***

"Fall and spring are the best times for group quilting," says Bea, standing in front of the stove as she takes off her coat. "Summer's too hot and sticky, and come winter, I don't like going out in the dark and cold."

"Well, speak for yourself," Ethel says. "Though my bones ache in the winter, there's nothing cozier to me than women sitting near a pot-bellied stove and quilting while the wind howls outside. I guess that's one of my earliest memories of winter—not the snow and ice, but the fire and the quilting bags. Mama, Aunt Maggie, and a few others used to entertain themselves telling stories while they stitched."

"What kind of stories?" asks Norma Jean. "Stories about people we know?"

"Well, some of them were made up tales, ghost stories and love stories and such. But lots of them were true. Or mostly true. You know how a story takes on color the more it's told. Some had been handed down from one generation to another; some were more recent, about folks who lived around here."

Norma Jean thinks of the silence she has grown up with, the stories she *hasn't* heard. She and Gram spent hours quilting by the fire when she was a child, but the only stories she has are the ones she dreams at night or makes up in her head.

"Well, personally,' Bea says, "I'm more interested in stories about what's happening to folks right now. You wouldn't believe what goes on in the lives of people you think you know. I mean *deacons* and *school teachers* and *young folks* that seem so pure. It's enough to make your hair curl."

"Now, Bea," says Miss Ella Mae, "gossip ain't *quite* the same thing as a story, though sometimes it gets stretched just as much. You see, there's things that you or someone reliable has seen with their own eyes and wants to tell about; then there's *gossip*, idle rumors about what *might* have happened. And then there's *stories*, people using their experiences, their memories and imagination, to reach down for something deeper and pass it on."

Maybe it's a story I'm looking for, Norma Jean thinks, the story of Julia, based on facts like the newspaper, but more, more than gossip, too. Enough little pieces of information that I can put them all together and *see* Julia's life—like watching a movie.

"I'd like to hear some of those stories you were talking about, Miss Ethel," Norma Jean says. "I always think how the cemetery is full

44

of stories, but no one to tell them. And I think of the stories that led up to *my* story. Gram couldn't tell them to me like your mama did."

Ethel looks up from the pieces of cloth she is sorting from the scrap bag. "Well, pretty soon Edna'll be making her special apple raisin pies. You bring me over a slice one day, and I'll swap you a story."

"All right," says Norma Jean, concentrating on her needle to hide the flush of pleasure she knows is showing on her face. "Sure."

***

Balancing a pie in her left hand, Norma Jean opens the gate to Ethel's yard. The strings from last summer's pea vines crisscross the side of the porch, and an old dog, large as the doormat he's lying on, raises his head sleepily, before going back to his dreaming. The Poseys, Ethel and Ivy (short for Ivan), have lived here as long as Norma Jean can remember, but she's never been inside. The house is small, an aging one-story building with a wrap-around porch like so many older places in town, but everything looks spruced up and clean. Ivy is the man folks call on to repair and fix anything, and she can tell, just by looking, that the screen door won't sag on its hinges or the porch swing creak.

Norma Jean hesitates at the bottom of the stair, unsure how to reach the door without disturbing the dog. Just as she's thinking of going around to the back, the door opens and Ethel calls out to her, nudging the dog aside.

"Come in, child, come on in. That looks like more than a slice of pie to me. Guess that means I'll have to share it with Ivy."

"Well," says Norma Jean shyly, "I made it myself, Miss Ethel. But Aunt Edna was in the kitchen the whole time to make sure I did it right."

Ethel takes the pie from her hands and Norma Jean follows her to the kitchen.

"Are you a cook, then, as well as a quilter?"

"Not really, but Aunt Edna's trained me to do everything she does at the house. She says it's important to know how."

45

"Well, that's the way it's always been done" says Ethel as she takes a couple of plates down from the shelf, "the older ones passing on what they know to those younger. Sure won't hurt you. Still, not everyone's cut out to be a homemaker, and Edna sets a high standard." She pauses, the coffee pot in her hand.

"It's like horses, you know. There are plow horses and riding horses and show horses. And you've got a balky animal on your hands if you try to make one do the job of another." Ethel smiles. "I don't think you're a plow horse, Norma Jean. And I can't see you prancing around the ring, either. But a good riding horse is a sight to behold, all strong and full of energy. 'Beauty in motion,' as they say."

"Miss Ethel, I don't think . . ."

"I know, I know. You're just a filly yet," Ethel laughed, "but these things show through. You'll see."

They sit at the table by the kitchen window eating warm pie and drinking coffee. Norma Jean looks out at the neat rows of fall vegetables in Ivy's garden and bright bursts of color from Ethel's chrysanthemums. How comfortable it feels, how simple and balanced. Directly behind her own house is the chicken yard, making it easier to feed the chickens and gather eggs. Practical but plain, with no thought of beauty.

"So," says Ethel, "a story. Or maybe for a whole pie I should say stories, old stories of Pine Grove. My great-grandfather was among the first settlers here, so there are stories that go way back."

"I wish so much that Gram could tell me stories like that. I know she didn't grow up in Pine Grove, but I don't even know how she and Grandpa met."

"Hmmm, let me see. I'm not sure about that, probably on a hayride. She's from the next county, you know, but she had a cousin used to live here and her family would come visiting once in a while. Hayrides were the big thing in those days for boys and girls getting together. Yes, several gals had their eye on Travis, him being so strong and having such a good farm and all. But none of them got a chance

46

once Aggie came along. Did you know she was only seventeen when they married? Just a little bit older than you."

"No, I didn't know. That's the trouble. I don't know enough to even imagine what they were like. I wonder if it was hard for her to move into a new place, even one as small as Pine Grove."

"Oh, no, not as far as us women were concerned. We all just loved her once she was here. She had one of those sweet personalities, you know. And she was fun. Always saw the humor in things. I think she must have been the easiest person alive to live with.

"Now, Travis, he could be touchy. He liked for things to go his way, even the weather. But she used to laugh when we were quilting and say, 'Travis is all in a tangle about something. I keep telling him, there are some knots that just won't give. Sometimes there's nothing for it but to cut the thread and start over.' She'd laugh that wonderful laugh of hers. It was funny 'cause we all knew Travis wasn't much good at letting go of *any*thing. She leaned on him though. I guess she always counted on him to keep things going like they should."

"Uncle Frank says Aunt Edna's a lot like him in some ways."

"Yes, I suppose she is. Always clear about what she's doing. And competent, too. With Frank's help she's stepped right in there to run the farm. She knew how to do about everything anyway."

"Was my mother more like Aggie? Was she like a young Gram?"

"No, I wouldn't say that exactly. Julia, well, Julia was an original. Not really like anyone I've ever known. She was fey, if you know what I mean, a bit eccentric, whimsical. Sometimes it seemed she belonged to a different world. She and Aggie were both lighthearted though, that I can say. You know, it's a shame," says Ethel, gazing out the window. "I've noticed that sometimes the lighthearted ones last only a short season, like butterflies. Without some sort of ballast, they don't keep going."

"So when Grandpa died, so unexpectedly and all, Aggie just fell apart?"

47

"No," Ethel looks out beyond the gardens, "I don't think so. She was all broke up, of course, and shocked. Everyone was; he was just in his fifties. But all in all, she weathered that pretty well, given the circumstances. It was Julia's death, coming so soon afterwards, that hit her hardest. I'm sorry, Norma Jean. I wish you could have known them all."

"Miss Ethel," Norma Jean begins in a tight voice, "what do you think happened to my mother?"

"I don't know, child. It's a mystery and all anyone can do is speculate. Aggie was very gentle with her that last year, the year you were born, soothing her in every way she could. But Julia had lost her spark. It was like she almost wasn't there anymore. You were the only thing she seemed to connect with, but her spirit was missing. It was a beautiful, free spirit. I see it in you, though different, of course, quieter and more thoughtful. She may have left her deepest part here in you."

CHAPTER 4

December is unusually cold, bitter at times. On sunny days, the stubble in the field sparkles with frost, and the cows stand close to each other blowing out their steamy breath. Gram, an afghan over her thin shoulders, a quilt over her knees, and a comforter tucked around her back, looks almost pudgy as she sits by the fire. Only her small head, hawk-like with its pulled-back gray hair and sharp black eyes, suggests her frail body.

The fire is so hot Norma Jean has to sit on the far side of the old woman's chair to feed her. As she lifts the spoon to her mouth, the flames' reflection dances in Gram's eyes, and for a moment she almost looks merry. Norma Jean's reminded of Ethel's remarks about Gram's sense of humor in times past. "Not the loud story-telling kind," she'd said, "but a real twinkle of laughter in her eyes whenever she was amused. And a lot of things seemed to amuse her. I declare, she was as light as Travis was solemn. A pair of opposites in that respect."

Uncle Frank throws more logs on the fire and sparks fly against the blackened stones. But Gram's expression doesn't change. She is way inside herself, thinks Norma Jean. How I'd love to go in there with her for a while, to know what she's thinking, see what she's seeing.

"Gram," she says, "would you like to know what *I'm* thinking? I'm making something up in the attic, something special about you and all the family. It's kind of a secret, but I'll show it to you when I'm finished. I think you'll like it."

Earlier that morning, Norma Jean had bundled up and gone to the attic. It was too cold up there to do much with her quilt pieces, but the sun was beaming on the ice-covered south windows. She wrapped herself in an old blanket and sat staring at them for a long time.

She could see nothing through them, only the silvery-white ice formed of thousands of droplets that gleamed brilliantly in the sunlight. Bright pinpoints of color—pink, blue, green—danced on the frosted pane, shifting and moving as she turned her head. Another aspect of the world seemed to be revealing itself. Not the familiar images of clouds and trees and fields, but something simultaneously clouded and radiant, frozen yet alive with mystery and color. Like looking at the stars, only closer, brighter. Like touching another universe.

As she gazed, fascinated, at the icy windowpane, it came to her that perhaps seeing clearly was not the only important thing. Perhaps there was another kind of seeing, momentary and surprising, eyes opened to the quickening radiance of light.

***

They stand in front of Logan's store in a cold January wind waiting for the school bus that will take them to Masontown for the game. Shirleen's father would have waited, letting them stay warm in the car, but she'd hopped out as soon as he stopped saying, "No thanks, Dad, we'll be fine." Now she babbles away, flushed with anticipation of the bus ride while Norma Jean hugs herself and jumps from foot to foot to stay warm.

"Come on, Norma Jean," she'd said. "Say you'll go. It's fun to ride the bus to a game, not at all like riding it to school. Everybody jokes and sings, and I know Buddy Ray will be going. I just *have* to go, but I can't go by myself."

"I don't really want to go, Shirleen. It'll take almost an hour to get to Masontown and that much again coming home. And all in the dark where you can't look out and see anything. It doesn't sound like much fun."

"But it *is* fun, Norma Jean, that's just what I'm saying. And there's lots of really cute guys in Masontown. You might see someone you'd like. Please say you'll go, please, please."

"How do you know Buddy Ray's even coming, Shirleen? He might have gotten a ride or something."

"I heard him say so—in the hall. He was talking some other guys into showing up, too. He'll be here."

A group of kids begins to collect around them, jostling and joking, occasionally letting out a cheer for the team. In the darkness they all seem strangely displaced, and the creaking, yellow bus, shifting gears as it turns the corner, is like something out of a dream.

Shirleen makes sure they are the first ones on board. She takes a window seat about half way down the aisle and motions Norma Jean to the one behind her. She's already said they shouldn't sit together. She wants the seat next to her free for Buddy.

Slowly the students fill the bus. A couple of girls try to take Shirleen's empty seat; also Wayne Pickens, an awkward, snub-nosed guy who's sweet on her, but she waves them away. "Sorry," she smiles brightly. "It's saved."

Finally Buddy Ray's head appears inside the door, and Shirleen turns in her seat. "There he is," she says, smoothing her hair. "Keep your fingers crossed."

He makes his way down the aisle, filling the space with his burly football player's body and slapping guys on the shoulder. His size and his confidence, magnified in the narrow dark passage of the bus, cause Norma Jean to shrink back, awed by his easy self-assurance. She can feel Shirleen holding her breath, about to burst with hope and excitement. He stops at her seat and she looks up at him.

"Hey, Shirleen," he says. "How's my study hall buddy? Say, do me a favor, will you? Go sit with Norma Jean so Janice and I can sit together?" Janice Rice pokes her head around his shoulder giggling as usual and smacking gum. Shirleen stares at Buddy, her mouth hanging open, for a few disbelieving moments. She looks down, the dim light mercifully hiding the flush that Norma Jean knows has spread over her face.

"Sure, sure," she says. Rising quickly she steps into the aisle and slides in the empty seat next to Norma Jean.

***

The game is slow and discouraging. Farm boys are playing farm boys, but the Masontown team is older, made up of seniors who have been playing together for four years. They seem to thwart most of Pine Grove's plays, and when they drive towards the goal, no one can stop them. The gym is overheated, steamy with bodies packed together on the hard wooden seats. When the home team scores a goal, the crowd cheers and stomps its feet in approval. The noise is deafening. In Masontown as in Pine Grove, everyone in town goes to the games on Friday night.

Shirleen acts like she's recovered from her disappointment about Buddy, although Norma Jean suspects she's just putting on a brave face. Her cheeriness and enthusiasm seem forced. But she goes along with it. She knows her friend avoids whatever she'd like to forget. She'd rather go on to the next thing than worry over what's past.

Shirleen's eyes rove over the crowd, especially the high seats where the guys sit, sideline coaches, calling out to the teams, imitating the cheerleaders, laughing out over some joke or comment as though they were lords of the gym. Norma Jean wonders for the hundredth time why Shirleen has to always have her sights set on some guy. In the opposite corner, a small section is roped off for the few coloreds that sometimes attend the games.

"Oh my gosh," says Shirleen, grabbing Norma Jean's arm. "Do you see him? There in the doorway, leaning against the wall. Who *is* he? He's terrific."

At the doorway left of the home goal, a dark-haired guy in blue jeans and a white tee shirt leans casually against the doorframe, hands stuffed into his tight jeans pockets, one black-booted foot crossed carelessly over the other. From where they sit she can see a pack of cigarettes rolled up in his shirt sleeve.

"He's too old, Shirleen. No high school kid would show his cigarettes. He doesn't even look like he belongs here."

"He looks great to me. Like Marlon Brando. A real man. Not like these silly high school boys. Let's go down at the half and meet him."

" Maybe that's not such a good idea. We'd seem like silly high school *girls*. Probably not his type."

"But Norma Jean, that's what makes it fun. And anyway, why would he be here if he didn't like high schoolers. Come on, I need your help. I just want to meet him."

When the buzzer sounds for half time, they make their way down the clunky wooden bleachers along with the crowd. Norma Jean wishes she hadn't come. She doesn't like going up to boys she doesn't know; it feels awkward, and she never knows what to say. Shirleen is so forward that Norma Jean's usually embarrassed for her. Yet, she wants to help her friend.

They finally reach the hallway and make their way down to the lower level where drinks are sold. Shirleen is searching the crowd like a hawk while Norma Jean silently hopes that "Marlon" has disappeared.

"Hi, Shirleen." The voice comes from behind them. "I thought that was you in the gym, but I couldn't get your attention."

A tall, freckled and friendly-looking guy smiles at them.

52

"Neill!" Shirleen says with surprise. "What are you doing here? I thought your family had left Masontown and moved to Jackson."

"Yeah, we moved, but my cousin Tim is center on the team so I usually make the games. Dad'll let me take the car anywhere to see Timmy. They're playing great this year. He's already got a scholarship to State."

While they're talking, Norma Jean is aware that Neill is talking to her as well as Shirleen. She feels the color rising in her face. Just at that moment he turns her way and smiles. A nice smile, so open and unguarded.

"Hi," he says. "I'm Neill, Neill Thompson. Saw you sitting next to Shirleen, but I don't know your name. You from Pine Grove, too?"

Norma Jean sends a pleading look to Shirleen who is eyeing the crowd around them. She swallows and opens her mouth to answer, but before she can speak, Shirleen interrupts.

"Listen, I have to run—to the bathroom. I might step out and have a cig, too. Can I leave you two together? Be back soon as I can, but you know how those lines are."

Norma Jean feels panicky. This guy doesn't even know her. But Shirleen is already making her way through the crowd and turning the corner, hurrying to get where she's going.

"Listen, you don't need to . . ."

"That Shirleen," he grins. "We got to be friends at church camp a couple of years ago. She's a lot of fun. But boy, can she talk. It's hard to get a word in edgewise. Let's get a Coke and sit down somewhere. You can fill me in on life in Pine Grove, what you do and all."

They move down to the end of the hall where some chairs have been pulled out from a classroom.

"Well," she says, looking down at her hands, "well, we live out from town, on a farm, and I, well, I help out. And I work at Logan's— you know, the general store there—on Saturdays, and, well, I guess I don't do very much." She is thinking how boring this must sound, but

53

when she glances up, Neill is looking right at her, smiling like it's really interesting.

"You know, this probably will sound silly, but the thing I've been doing this year, I mean that excites me, is my quilt. I'm making a really different sort of quilt."

"Is that so?" His smile widens and she notices that his eyes are green, clear green, like Coke bottle glass. "Where'd you get the idea for that?"

Before she can answer, the buzzer sounds ending the halftime break. Looking down the hallway, she sees a short line still extending from the Ladies room.

"Let's go up," says Neill. "We'll sit in your seats. She'll find us. I want you to see my cousin in the game."

Norma Jean is amazed at how interesting the game is when you're with someone who knows something about it. Neill's cousin is fast and graceful for a big guy. When he runs down the court and jumps to shoot, he almost seems to be flying. Neill tells her who to watch as they're setting up a play, and at some point she begins to see the teamwork. From where they sit in the bleachers, the game is like moving pieces, coming together and moving apart in a pattern, the ball being the thread that connects it. But all happening so fast, like the quickly assembling pieces in a kaleidoscope.

Before she knows it the buzzer is signaling the end of the third quarter—and still no sign of Shirleen.

"I'm going to find her," she says, rising. "Maybe she got sick or something. I better go see."

She's surprised when he wants to come with her, but also glad. It's not like Shirleen to stay away from the crowd. The downstairs hall is pretty empty now, and there's no sign of her in the Ladies. Outside then, smoking. But for a whole quarter? They pull on their coats, bundling up against the cold night air, and push open the heavy door.

54

Norma Jean blinks in the bright light above the doorway. A handful of men stand nearby having their between-quarter smoke. Beyond the circle of light there is only the blackness of cedar trees moaning in the gusty wind. Off to the right a tarred path leads down to the parking lot, its descent illuminated by a single naked bulb on a wooden pole.

"I don't see her." Norma Jean looks from side to side.

"Well, if she's smoking, she wouldn't be right here. You're suspended if they catch you on school grounds. Kids usually go back in the trees and hide the glow with their hand. Or she might have gone to the parking lot if, well, if she wasn't alone."

Norma Jean stiffens and a shudder creeps up her back. "Neill, she wanted to meet this guy she saw across the gym. But he was older, kind of tough looking. I hope she didn't . . ."

"Come on, we'll go down there. There's a flashlight in my car. Don't worry, we'll find her."

Flashlight in hand, they weave in and out among the cars calling Shirleen's name. Neill leads the search and systematically they cover the parking lot, looking carefully, but not talking much. The muffled sound of a cheer coming from the gym seems remote as a passing train. Norma Jean pulls her coat together as a sense of foreboding sweeps through her .

Neill holds out a hand of caution, then hits the roof of a dark blue sedan with his fist. Two heads pop up, their startled, angry expressions caught in the flashlight's beam, but neither of them is Shirleen. The parking lot yields nothing.

"O.K.," says Neill, motioning the flashlight toward the trees. "We better try there. We'll get help if we don't find her."

She's immensely grateful for Neill's presence, the way he knows what to do and the way he seems to care. What would she do by herself? She doesn't want to report Shirleen missing, get her in trouble. They head towards the old cedars. There's no path to follow. Even with the flashlight, they move slowly into the darkness. Twice Norma Jean

55

stumbles on a gnarled root; only Neill's quick reaction keeps her from falling, Gusts of wind blow low branches into their faces. She feels completely disoriented and is close to panic when finally they hear a whimper. Neill turns the light to the base of a big tree, and they see Shirleen. She's curled up in a ball by the trunk, hugging her stomach and rocking. One leg sticks out from her skirt, and Norma Jean gasps at the bare foot, so white and exposed in the cold night. Her coat is pulled down around the elbows and her hair, full of debris, hangs over her face.

"Oh, no," Norma Jean gasps, her hand covering her mouth. For a moment she's afraid she'll throw up and reaches out blindly for Neill's arm.

"Shirleen," she says. "Oh, Shirleen."

They drop down beside her. Norma Jean pulls the coat up over her shoulders and strokes her back. "It's all right, it's all right. We're here now, Neill and I are here. Tell us what happened. How bad are you hurt?"

Shirleen breaks into heavy sobs, her whole body shaking as though all her cells were crying together. Neill takes off his coat and tucks it around her. She won't look up, but holds Norma Jean's hands in a tight grip as they wait for the sobs to lessen.

"Oh, Norma Jean, it was awful—awful. You were right about him, you were right. What will I do? I don't want anyone to see me."

"Can you tell us what happened, Shirleen? Did he . . . did he hit you or . . . or . . . force you? Where are you hurt?"

Norma Jean lifts Shirleen's hair out of her eyes and sees an ugly red welt on the side of her face. Her stomach churns at the sight. Everything in her wants to be somewhere else—in the attic, in the hayloft, in the safety of the quilting circle with wise and patient women.

"I can't tell you now," Shirleen whispers with a glance toward Neill and grasps Norma Jean's hand even tighter.

For a few moments they sit there, Shirleen's head in Norma Jean's lap, Neill hunched against the cold and holding the flashlight to one side, bathing them in its faint glow. Nothing moves but the wind. Nothing is heard but its whooshing sound and the creaking of limbs. The world seems far away, the three of them held in a strange tableau.

A strong gust hits them and Neill rises. "I'm going to get help, a doctor or something—and the sheriff. I saw him at the game."

"NO!" Shirleen says, sitting up for the first time. "No, please don't call anyone. Please, Neill. I don't want anyone to come. I couldn't stand it. I couldn't."

"But Shirleen . . ." Norma Jean's eyes fill with tears; she finds it hard to talk. "We need to make sure you're all right. A nurse or someone needs to check you."

"No. No. No." Shirleen pleads, wiping her face. "No, I don't want that. Please, Norma Jean, I don't want that. It's just that I can't go home, not tonight. They'd know something was wrong."

Norma Jean looks up at Neill. The ground feels hard and cold and the game will soon be over. They can't remain here.

"You can come to my house, Shirleen. They'll be in bed when we get there. We can go right up to my room."

Looking up anxiously, Shirleen nods a reluctant assent.

"Come on then." Neill leans down to help her to her feet. "I'll drive you there. We'll tell the bus driver you're sick. And call your folks. It'll be easier to think in the morning, to figure out what to do."

One on each side, they help Shirleen, who walks slowly, her eyes downcast, toward the parking lot.

"You really need to report that guy, Shirleen," Neill says, "whatever he did. He needs to pay. But it's up to you to decide."

They drive home in silence, Shirleen huddled in a corner of the back seat, every now and then emitting a muffled sob. Norma Jean sits up front with Neill feeling awkward and worried, feeling more things than she can sort out, but not wanting to upset Shirleen who has her legs folded up to her chin, her arms wrapped around them, holding them tightly in place like a shield. When they finally reach the farm, Neill helps her out of the car.

"Get some rest, Shirleen, Let Norma Jean take care of you." He nods her way, lightly squeezing her arm. "I'll call you tomorrow."

Shirleen stays a long time in the bathroom, but refuses Norma Jean's help. Once in the single bed, she turns her face to the wall, pulls her knees up again to her chest and slowly rocks herself back and forth. In a short time, however, the rocking stops and Norma Jean can tell by her breathing that, at least for now, she's fallen into an exhausted sleep.

She sighs with relief and has one thought—to get to the attic where she can calm down and think. It'll be cold up there, but she has her coat and warm blankets. The cold will feel crisp and clarifying, and that's what she needs.

***

They drop Shirleen off at her house the next morning when Uncle Frank drives Norma Jean to Logan's for work. She squeezes her friend's hand as she leaves the truck.

"Take it easy; you can stay in bed all weekend. Just tell them you're sick." Shirleen stares at her dully and sighs.

"She don't seem like herself," Uncle Frank comments as they pull away.

"Yeah, must be coming down with the flu or something."

CHAPTER 5

The store is busy, as it usually is on Saturdays when all the country people come to town to do their week's shopping, sell and trade their wares, visit with each other. Their talk buzzes around her like a swarm of muffled bees. Norma Jean focuses on her tasks—cutting straight lines across the cloth with the large store scissors, wrapping packages up in brown paper and string. She tries to block the brutality of last night from her mind, but she keeps seeing the look on Shirleen's face. Revulsion and compassion fill her heart.

There's another feeling, small but steady and rising in the foreground, a quiet excitement she's ashamed to admit in the midst of Shirleen's trouble. Neill.

Boys, boyfriends haven't been much a part of her life. The ones she knows seem too silly, too loud and rough, with their horseplay and their boasting. Not that she hasn't star-gazed, imagined the perfect guy that might one day come along—a dreamy vision, far removed from the flesh and blood guys in her everyday world.

"Hi," says a voice over the counter. She looks up with a start into green eyes. "I called your house," says Neill. "They said you were here . . . working." He shifts his feet, hands stuffed in his pockets. "Dad needed me to do a delivery over this way." He smiles. "Well, actually, about ten miles closer to Jackson—but I'll refill the tank."

Norma Jean smiles back briefly and ducks her head, pleased to see him, but embarrassed to be seen by the others. "Good. I'm . . . I'm glad to see you, I really am. But I can't talk now. I mean, you know, I'm working and this is the busiest day." She glances toward Miss Logan at the front of the store and blushes in confusion.

"It's O.K., I know you're busy. Wish I could hang around till you get off, but I'm working, too. For my old man. At the drug store. I was calling to ask about tomorrow. Could I come over after church? I could see your farm, meet your folks and all."

Norma Jean feels a moment of panic. What will she say to Aunt Edna? How will she explain? What will they think?

"Will you be home?"

"Well, yeah, sure—after church and all."

"Good," he nods, "see you then."

She turns to a customer who's asking to see a bolt of brown corduroy; when she turns back, he's gone, quickly as he came.

On the counter next to the cash register, Norma Jean sees a neatly printed sign:

A CLINIC FOR PINE GROVE ?

Tired of driving or finding a ride to Jackson to see a doctor?
Want our children and elders to get important regular check-ups?
Pine Grover's deserves the same available medical attention as City Folk.
Join the CLINIC COMMITTEE and help to make this possible!
Contact Ethel Posey at phone # 707 or PO Box # 400

Norma Jean smiles. Ethel said she'd wanted to be a nurse. Now, in her own way, she's still trying to bring health to the community.

***

Norma Jean calls Shirleen after work. She's been in bed all day and sounds listless. "Mama's stepped out for a minute, else she wouldn't let me come to the phone. You know how she is. I told them the mark on my face was from a branch I ran into in the dark, and that I felt like I was getting the flu or something. She won't let me out of the bed, but I don't feel like doing anything anyway. I don't even feel like talking so don't call again, Norma Jean. I don't know when I'll get back to school."

***

At breakfast Norma Jean takes a deep breath and says someone's coming by after church—a friend of Shirleen's she met at the game Friday night. Aunt Edna peers at her over the top of her glasses. "Is this the boy that called here for you yesterday?"

Norma Jean nods and focuses on her cereal. She imagines Uncle Frank and Aunt Edna exchanging looks across the table.

"Well, good," says Uncle Frank. "He'll be welcome."

They're just finishing Sunday dinner when Norma Jean hears the car coming slowly up the drive. She hesitates, not sure if she should go out on the porch to greet him or wait until he knocks. Before she can decide, Uncle Frank is heading up the hall and opening the door. She sees them shaking hands at the foot of the steps and waits as he waves Neill on back to the kitchen. Neill grins broadly when he sees her and hands Aunt Edna a pint of ice cream as Norma Jean mumbles out an introduction.

"From my dad's drugstore," he says.

"Well, isn't that nice," says Aunt Edna. "Just what we need to go with our apple pie." Norma Jean is surprised at her cordiality as she motions him to take a seat at the table.

The visit is a great success. It's fun showing Neill the barn, Bessie's stall that needs fresh straw every day, and the chicken house where he watches her reach under a hen and "magically" pull out an egg. He's amazed at the varieties of chickens—bronze, reddish, black and white speckled. He asks so many questions, she has to laugh. Though there are farms all over the county, she realizes that Neill really is a town boy.

***

On Monday when Shirleen's not in school, Norma Jean feels at a loss about what to do. She writes her a long note about school stuff hoping to cheer her up. She doesn't mention anything about Friday night for fear her mother will read it. And she doesn't say anything about Neill either, in case that might remind her of what happened. She has no idea how she would feel in Shirleen's situation, or what she would do. But Shirleen can't withdraw forever; maybe she just needs a little time.

***

When she was in the library looking at the March, 1936 issues of *The County Bulletin*, Norma Jean knew she could also have asked for those of September 1935, the month of her grandfather's death. I'll do that sometime, she'd thought, but not now. She's not drawn to Travis. He sounds harsh and forceful; she never thinks of him as "Grandpa." She doubts she would've been comfortable in his presence.

Yet he is part of her heritage, too, this rough man who knew farming, who could manage animals, plow the fields and make crops

61

grow. Perhaps he was like the other Taylor farmers before him, and she pictures a series of stocky men with wind-burned faces, their heavy work boots rattling the floorboards as they stomp on the back porch to knock off clods of mud.

It's hard to fit this image into the picture she's developing of Julia and a younger Gram. Of course Uncle Frank is also a farmer, but he's different, a quiet, gentle sort of man, easy and at home in the barn and the fields, as much in his element as the cows in the pasture.

Norma Jean looks over the quilt fabric she's been assembling in the attic. She doubts there's anything that represents Travis. Aunt Edna gave away all the clothes in the house that might remind Gram of her husband or daughter, and Norma Jean doesn't want to ask her about clothes in the attic. But there are overalls hanging in the barn. She's seen them on a hook next to the corn crib, though never on Uncle Frank. Things accumulate in a barn over the years the way they accumulate in an attic—old tools, ropes, bits of machinery left in place to rust and gather dust just in case they might one day come in handy. A hold-over from earlier times when farm supply stores and catalogues and money itself were not readily available.

She picks up her scissors and heads toward the barn. The aroma of straw and manure reminds her of how she used to love playing here, talking to the cows and the horses they had then, searching for new litters of kittens born in a dark corner or under the floorboards. She runs her hand over the old gray planks of the corn crib door, her fingers remembering the rough places and the smooth.

The overalls are still there, stiff with age and rotting around the bottom of the legs. She holds them out and is surprised at their large size, huge really. Maybe they were meant to be put on over other clothes. She pulls the ragged cuff downward and cuts off first one leg, then the other. On an impulse, she carries them up to the loft, retrieving the hidden billfold on the way. Sitting on a bale of hay, the pant legs in her lap, she takes out the picture. Here they are, the mystery people, her closest dead ancestors. She studies both of them as though she could will some answers to come through. Slapping the pieces of overalls against the barn wall to shake loose some of the dust and rolling them up into a tight bundle, she returns the photo to its place and heads for the basement washtub.

***

Norma Jean has made up her mind to try completing the quilt face by graduation. The idea of overlays, one piece of fabric overlapping or spinning off of another, excites her. What began as a salve for her loneliness and confusion has taken on new life constantly surprising her. She could never have planned this design ahead of time, not in a hundred years. But she's learning to trust the unfolding of the quilt, and in the lightness of spirit this gives her, she is feeling more trustful of her own unfolding.

Most people, she's sure, will think the quilt strange, even ugly. And she almost laughs imagining Aunt Edna's expression when she sees it, the way her eyes bug out when she's shocked or dismayed. The uneven blocks of background fabric, the irregular crossings and circular overlays of such odd and various materials will confound her. Order and regularity are her cornerstones. But Norma Jean loves the way it's looking. And it's fascinating how the pieces of cloth themselves let her know where they need to be.

She hasn't been able to keep the quilt a surprise as she'd hoped because she wants to have clothing scraps from those who live in the house now, Aunt Edna, Uncle Frank, Gram and herself. Norma Jean tells them at supper one night in late February about her special project in the attic, a family quilt, and she needs something from each of them to include.

Uncle Frank is amused and says he never expected he would end up in a quilt. Aunt Edna's non-committal, but she comes back that evening with an old yellow apron she doesn't wear much anymore, and a blue and white plaid shirt Uncle Frank wears around the farm but has really outgrown. From Gram's drawer Norma Jean takes a lace-trimmed eyelet collar that she'd loved seeing around Gram's neck when she was a child and sat by her chair as she quilted. Her own piece of cloth is still undecided.

63

The work is going pretty fast now. Every week at the quilting circle she brings out pieces to work with and in the attic she's begun to stitch them together. The women are curious about the odd- shaped pieces, but they withhold their comments and questions. Bea frequently rolls her eyes or shakes her head, but the quiet of Miss Ella Mae and Ethel Posey keeps her silent. Although the group has the custom of working together to help each other with the quilting once the quilt face is done, Norma Jean's not sure about that. It would get it finished much faster, but she might want to do this one by herself.

***

At quilting circle that week Ethel brings in one of her Clinic announcements.

"I just want to share this with you, though you've probably already seen it at Logan's. Having a clinic here's been a dream of mine a long time. We have to go to Jackson for all our doctoring and that's not so bad if you have a car in the family. But lots of folks don't. I'm thinking of old ones, like us . . ." she laughs and nods at Ella Mae, "and those who live alone—and the colored. They look out for each other with home remedies and such, but most can't afford a doctor in town."

"Well, a clinic would be handy for mothers, too." says Bea. "I hate carting those boys into Jackson for every ear ache and such—and having to drive Charlie to work *first* just to use the car. But who would *pay* for this clinic, hiring a doctor and all? And how could colored people be let in? We can't use the same waiting room and rest rooms, even if they only come one day a week. And nobody in Pine Grove's going to cough up that kind of money. No, it's a good idea, Miss Ethel, but it'll never happen."

"It's a *real* good idea, Ethel," Ella Mae says "possible, even if *not* probable. Have you been to the churches, the PTAs and such? We could even make baby quilts for the newborns if it had a birthing place. I'd be glad to help out in spreading the word. But that reminds me," she smiles at everyone, "there's something I want to show you before we leave."

64

She reaches behind her chair and pulls out a small quilt—crib-sized—a blue background with bright-colored birds flying across the surface, a big sun shining in one corner and green grass in another.

"When did you do this, Ella Mae?" asks Ethel. "Is there another grandchild on the way?"

"Look at those tiny stitches," Norma Jean says. "This quilt will last through a lot of children!"

Ella Mae smiles. "Well, I can't take any credit for it. But, if you was wanting to sell it, what do you think it's worth?"

The women are surprised by her question; most of their quilts are made as gifts.

"Well," says Bea, "if I had made that quilt, I think I'd want at least $25 for it."

"I don't know," Ethel says thoughtfully. "Think of all the hours it took to make it! $50 wouldn't be too much to ask. 'Course what you can *ask*, and what you can *get*, are two different things."

"I could imagine this selling for $75 or $80 in the city," Ella Mae says. "Minnie Lewis knocked on my back door the other day and asked if I'd like to buy it for $20. You all know her, don't you? She lives down there in colored town—takes in washing and does a beautiful job of ironing. She's raising her daughter Lavinia's children and trying to scrape out a living to feed them. I told her I wouldn't buy it for $20, but I'd help her get twice that much or more. I'm thinking of that shop over in Jackson, *Home Spun* I think it's called."

***

From the time she began working on this quilt, Norma Jean pictured the love pocket being in the center, everything else radiating out from it. Now she sees it shifting, as though it doesn't belong in so obvious a place. After all, she thinks, a regular pocket is often hidden in a seam or attached underneath the surface. Even when it's obvious like a patch pocket, the contents themselves are hidden.

When she first discovered the beautiful quilt square, and Miss Ella Mae described love pockets, she looked for an opening where a trinket or a note might be hidden. Nothing appeared. Now she holds the pocket in her hands feeling both sides. There must be something like that here, something secret and special. Of course to be truly hidden, the opening would be sewn up, stitched back together to hide the contents from sight. Is it foolish to open the seams to look? Where would she start?

She turns the pocket round and round, feeling the jewels of color—satin, taffeta, velvet. Any section could be a hiding place. Then one piece catches her eye, soft and velvety, the orangey pink hue of peace roses, a color echoed in the overlapping roses of the border. Slowly, carefully, she snips a stitch and gently tugs loose a few threads along the base of the triangle. When the opening is large enough for a finger, she reaches inside. At first it feels empty, only cloth a bit frayed with age. But when she moves her finger side to side, the texture is puzzling—thread-like, but different from thread. Odd.

She pulls back her forefinger and loosens a few more stitches, noticing how perfect they are, small and even. Pushing two fingers into the opening and using them like pincers, she takes hold of something and slowly withdraws her hand. "Oh," she gasps. Between her fingers are several long strands of hair.

Time seems to stop, along with her pulse and her breathing. Quickly she removes the rest of the stitches along the edge, reaches into the apex of the triangle and removes the contents. One jet black curl and a lock of brown hair tied together with crimson thread.

She holds them in her palm, tears fill her eyes. Her fingers stroke the separate locks, feeling their texture, soft as down. She lifts them up to the light where they catch the sun's gleam. How amazing, she thinks, how amazing. Here are my father and mother, the young man and woman who gave me life. I'm holding them in the palm of my hand.

And something more is here, too, something wonderful. She can't name what it is, but it feels bigger than even her and her parents.

She sits looking into her palm for a long time, her other hand unconsciously lifting and stroking strands of her own hair.

***

Shirleen stays away from school for a week and Norma Jean is glad to see her back. But she's quieter. Those gray eyes that were always so wide with anticipation, now look lifeless and wary.

"You're not ashamed, are you, Shirleen? It wasn't your fault; you have nothing to be ashamed about."

"Please, Norma Jean, I don't want to talk about it. I want to forget it, the whole thing, O.K.? I know you're trying to help, so that's the best way."

***

Several weeks later Norma Jean is on her way to meet Shirleen. It's a beautiful day in March; green shoots are pushing up in every garden she passes and dogwood trees are about to burst open in blossom. Inside Norma Jean a tiny bubble, iridescent and weightless, bounces and dances with each step. Neill. He's been to the farm several times, and seems to enjoy their country life. Twice he's picked her up to go to the movies in Jackson, though it meant two round trips for him. And recently they spent an afternoon walking through Ferris Park on the edge of the city, talking and laughing, breathing in the fresh spring air.

She hasn't met his folks yet, but she's sure she will soon. They'd driven past his father's pharmacy, but not gone in. Neill's father doesn't like him to bring friends in just to chat. And his mother has been worn out lately helping to care for a sick neighbor who lives alone. She wonders what they look like and who Neill resembles.

But when she arrives at the cemetery, she's surprised to see Shirleen already there, sitting on a stone bench near a tall granite marker. She looks so different with her shoulders hunched over, her head down, that Norma Jean hesitates and feels her exuberance sliding away.

"Shirleen?" she says, sitting on the bench beside her. Cold dampness from the stone moves up through her jeans like the chill of a hundred graves, and she turns toward her friend with apprehension. Shirleen looks downward, at nothing, both hands wrapped around the bench's rough edge, rocking herself nervously back and forth.

"I'm in trouble, Norma Jean. The worst kind of trouble. I don't know what to do."

Norma Jean stares, her mouth open but speechless. She knows she must say something. But nothing comes. The sight of Shirleen so still and serious alarms her as much as her words.

"Do you mean . . . do you mean that . . ."

Shirleen nods quickly, her hands grasping the stone even tighter. "Yes," she says, "yes." Her eyes are wide and pleading. "No one suspects, no one knows but you. I haven't told anyone."

"Oh, Shirleen, Shirleen." She reaches out to take her hand. How awful this must be, to know and have no one to tell.

Shirleen's eyes fill with tears and she collapses into Norma Jean's lap like an injured child, sobs of despair shaking her whole body.

Norma Jean smoothes her hair and lets her cry. She looks out over the cemetery, numbed by her own inadequacy to help or suggest anything. Her eyes fall in the direction of her mother's grave and she realizes, with a start, that Julia might have sat here, her arms on her stomach, and wondered what to do about the baby inside.

"You have to tell them, you know. Your parents. You need their help, Shirleen. They'd want to know."

"Oh, no." Shirleen sits up abruptly and grasps Norma Jean's hands. "They wouldn't want to know, they wouldn't. They'd be too upset—and ashamed. They'd have no idea what to do."

Norma Jean pictures Mrs. Miller puttering around her kitchen, ironing shirts and blouses in her housecoat and slippers while she listens to radio episodes of *Ma Perkins* and *Portia Faces Life*. She has heard her whiney "Now, Shirleen," as she makes a weak effort to corral the

68

behavior of her late-life child. A weary woman, weary and tiresome. It's like all the spunk in the family has funneled into Shirleen.

Mr. Miller works in the lumber mill halfway to Jackson and spends evenings reading the *Saturday Evening Post* or listening to the ball game. They both adore and ignore this child who was dropped into their midlife like a spirited puppy they're helpless to train.

"I've thought of going to see someone . . . you know, that woman that lives back in the woods near Brown's crossroads. They say that's what Clara Chumley did, and didn't miss a day of school. But I'm scared. I'm not sure I can do it, even if you and Neill go with me. It may be too late, anyway."

Norma Jean stares at her, dumbfounded. How does Shirleen know all this stuff—an old woman back in the woods? Clara Chumley? And what would Neill have to do with any of this? She feels a wave of fear in her own stomach.

"Look, Shirleen," she squeezes her friend's hands, "don't do anything yet. Let me think who could help. You're too upset to think straight right now."

The panicky look returns to Shirleen's face. "But I've already waited too lo . . . ," she wails.

"I know, I know. But one more day won't hurt, will it? I'll meet you here tomorrow, O.K.? Try to keep calm. Something'll work out."

***

Norma Jean leaves Shirleen in the cemetery and heads down Maple Street, avoiding the main street of town with its storefronts and passersby, folks stopping to talk or tooting a horn in a greeting as they did every day, as though all was right with the world. She's glad she planned to walk home. The three miles to the farm will give her time to think.

Something'll work out. That's what she'd said to Shirleen, words to soothe her turmoil. But what *could* work out? Norma Jean has no idea. She knows she is out of her depth, trying to save a friend

69

struggling in water when she herself can barely paddle. These last years her whole attention has been backward, tracing the streams and eddies that created her own pool of existence. Stitch by stitch it's taking shape in the form of her quilt, but this—Shirleen's desperation, her not knowing what to do, her fear of being found out and what it might lead her to—this is different. It's huge and real, and right in front of them—life-threatening, maybe life destroying, for both Shirleen and the baby. Something has to be done—soon.

She remembers the time when she was six or seven and Bessie, her favorite cow, was birthing a calf. There was a terrible storm, wind and rain and sharp cracks of lightning. Uncle Frank and Aunt Edna woke her up to sit with Gram, who startled at any loud sound. Norma Jean was frightened. She didn't want to be in the house alone. She was afraid they'd go out in the dark and never come back, get struck by the lightning or washed away and drowned.

"Wait," she cried. "Wait till the storm is over."

Aunt Edna moved on out the door, but Uncle Frank had stooped to her level and placed his hands on her shoulders.

"It *can't* wait, Norma Jean. Some things can't wait. Bessie needs us now. And Gram needs *you*. You'll do fine."

And she had—because they needed her to.

Now Shirleen needs her. And *she* needs to talk to someone who will know how to help. But who? Aunt Edna would have a practical suggestion. She's good in a crisis. But Norma Jean knows she can't trust her to keep it from Shirleen's parents. The more she thinks about it, the more she's sure Aunt Edna would say it's her duty to tell them.

She can trust Uncle Frank, no doubt about that. But she can't imagine talking to him about such things. How would she ever have the nerve to tell him? What would he know to do anyway? And Shirleen would be mortified.

Neill knows what happened. He was there that night. But she and Neill are just getting to know each other. No, she doesn't want to bring Neill into this.

Dismayed, she reaches Black River Road, the way to the farm. She's about to turn onto it when Ethel's face comes to mind, kind, wise Ethel whom they can surely trust.

***

Norma Jean finds Ethel standing in the yard surveying her daffodils. Their yellow trumpets form a thick border along the fence and walkway announcing a new season of life.

"Come in, come in," says Ethel opening the gate. "You're all I need to complete this picture of spring in bloom."

Norma Jean smiles weakly but doesn't respond as Ethel grasps her hand and spends a moment looking at her face.

"You're troubled, aren't you? Let's go get a cup of tea and talk about it."

Sitting in Ethel's kitchen, holding the steaming cup of tea in her hands and looking out over the rows of tiny vegetables pushing through the earth in the back garden, she starts to feel better, even though nothing has changed.

"Ethel," she says looking around. "It's so nice here, so peaceful. Has your life always been like this?"

Ethel smiles. "Nobody's life is *always* like anything, honey. We've had ups and downs. Why, when I was your age, I wanted worse than anything to be a nurse. I'd read stories about Clara Barton, and we had a visiting nurse in the county that had the prettiest smile. I wanted to be just like her. But there wasn't money for that kind of training."

"At least you knew what you wanted to be."

Ethel nods her head. "That's true, but the hardest time for me was the three babies I lost. If I couldn't be a nurse, I was going to be the *best* mother. That didn't work out either. I just couldn't seem to carry them to term, and after the last one they had to fix me so I couldn't even try anymore." She looks out at her back garden. "That's when I turned to flowers—and quilting. Ever notice how much a garden looks like a quilt when everything's in bloom?" She laughs. "And caring for a

71

garden, specially when you're just getting started, takes as much care and trouble as a batch of young'uns."

She stops talking and looks thoughtfully at Norma Jean. "Are you that worried about your future, honey?"

Norma Jean blushes and feels the tears welling up. "I don't know about my future. It's all so hazy I try *not* to think about it, though I guess I should. But I am worried, Ethel, worried about someone else's future, a friend of mine who needs help. I promised her I wouldn't tell anyone, but I'm afraid she might harm herself. And I don't know *how* to help her."

"I see," Ethel says, nodding and patting her hand. "You don't want to break your promise, but you don't want to stand by and do nothing when you see a friend too upset to use good judgment. That's a tough one. Maybe if we talk it over, you and I can figure out a way to help her. I can tell you this, Norma Jean, I won't do or say anything we don't agree on—unless it seems to seriously threaten someone's life."

Just hearing Ethel's reassuring voice calms Norma Jean's fears. She takes a deep breath and begins. "This friend of mine's in bad trouble. She's, you know, well, she's pregnant." Norma Jean looks down as she feels the color rising in her face. "It wasn't her fault, not really. This guy, he forced himself on her. And she won't tell her folks, she's too scared, too ashamed, I guess. She says she's going to . . . to get rid of it some way, a way that might kill her."

Ethel listens quietly, nodding her head now and then. "Well, you have good reason to be concerned, Norma Jean. There *is* a woman out in the country, an older woman who delivers most of the colored babies around here—no formal training, of course; she learned midwifing from her mother who had learned it from *her* mother before. Folks trust her to know what she's doing. And they go to her, too, when they don't want to have a baby born. I've never heard anything against her. But what your friend probably *doesn't* know is there's other choices. Thank goodness there are because she's not the only young girl that's found herself in this situation."

72

Ethel tells her of a place she knows a couple of counties away where Shirleen could go and live with other young women in the same predicament. Where they would take care of her and find a good home for the baby. The nurse that Ethel had admired and wanted to be like had started it, and they'd named it for her after she died, the *Anna Farraday Home for Young Women*. But she'd have to tell her parents, that's the only way she could go.

Norma Jean sighs. "I don't think she'll tell them."

"Well," says Ethel, "I can understand her not wanting to do that, but if it's who I'm thinking, I could talk to them, too, after your friend does. There's ways you can put things that help people feel better about them." She pauses for a moment, then smiles. "I've known Pearl Miller all her life. We're not close friends, mind you, but we've been in the same church circle for years. Shirleen's talking about going away to college anyway, so no one ever needs to know."

Norma Jean leaves Ethel's feeling hopeful. But encouraged as she is, there's a deep heaviness in all this, a dark place lodged somewhere in her chest, sad as despair. Her mind keeps going to the baby growing in Shirleen's body, quietly, blindly uncurling as naturally as a daffodil. But no one awaiting its arrival, no homeplace waiting at all.

CHAPTER 6

Three days pass before Norma Jean and Shirleen can get together again. First Shirleen's sick, then it pours rain, drenching the fields and churning up the river till it roars under the bridge like a herd of horses. On the telephone Norma Jean mentions hopeful news, but she's afraid to say more. The phone is in the hallway in the middle of the house.

Now she approaches the cemetery, eager to share Ethel's suggestion. Shirleen arrives a few minutes later walking briskly. Something is different. Before she can say anything, Shirleen grabs her hands and pulls her down to the bench.

"Listen," she says, "I've got an idea—Neill. Neill and I could cross the state line and get married. Then my parents won't be so upset."

"What?" Norma Jean gasps, "marry Neill? That's crazy. Neill's going off to college in the fall. He won't agree to it anyway. It's not *his* baby."

"No, listen. Neill and I are old friends. He covered for me once at church camp when I stayed out with a boy after hours. I think he'll do it. He was there, he knows how it happened. And he's keen on helping people, like it's his *calling* or something. See, we'd be married, have the license and everything. Then we'd get it annulled, our parents could do that, and Neill could go off to college, and I'd put the baby up for adoption soon as it's born."

Norma Jean stares at her, dumbfounded at such a stupid idea. And something else, something hot and angry flares up inside her. She takes a deep breath.

"Shirleen, this is *not* a good idea. Think of Neill for a minute, how it would make *him* look, what his parents would say. He won't do it anyway. He won't lie. You shouldn't even ask him. But listen, I have another idea, one that would also end in adoption."

As Norma Jean unfolds Ethel's plan, Shirleen frowns and shakes her head.

"No. No. I can't do that. I can't tell them I'm pregnant without a husband. They'd demand to know who the father is, I know them, they would. They'd mope around and read the Bible to me and make me feel awful. And I don't want to be in a *home* with a lot of trashy girls. Low life, Norma Jean. That's who goes to those places. Why did you *tell* Ethel when you knew I didn't want *anyone* to know?"

Norma Jean throws up her hands in exasperation. "You don't have a lot of choices, Shirleen. I understand you don't want anyone to know, but everyone's going to know when you start showing. Why don't you go talk to Ethel? I'll go with you. You have the wrong idea about *Farraday*."

74

Shirleen stands up and crosses her arms on her chest. Her face is dark and stubborn. "I know what I'm going to do. I'm going to take a trip to the woods. I'll ask Neill to take me there and bring me back. If he won't do the married thing, maybe he'll do this. You don't have to come, Norma Jean. It's not your problem."

Norma Jean springs to her feet. "You can't do that Shirleen, you can't. It's not safe, it'll cost money—and what about the baby. Have you thought one moment about that tiny, defenseless baby? Why, that could be *me* inside my mother. Suppose *she* had gone to that old woman in the woods? Think about that."

"*You* think about it, Norma Jean. We can't ask her, can we?" Shirleen says gesturing towards Julia's grave. "She had the baby and then went crazy and drowned herself. I'm doing what's best for *me*."

Shirleen strikes off across the cemetery, tromping over grave mounds, flowering bulbs, anything in her path to the street. The weight in Norma Jean's chest is about to explode. Her eyes brim with tears ready to gush forth, but a scream wells up inside her, the anger and betrayal of Shirleen's words, her friend, her best and only friend whom she's trying to help—how could she? How could she say such things about her mother—that she was crazy, that getting pregnant and having a baby, having *her*, had caused her to drown.

Her body shakes with an onslaught of feelings. She stamps her foot into the spongy turf. She kicks the nearest tombstone. Her teeth bite hard on her lower lip. Pounding her legs with closed fists, she walks the cemetery in a heat, crunching the gravel path, grinding it in with her heel.

Third time round, she begins to breathe easier and slows her pace. She notices wild violets sprinkled here and there in the grass. What a quiet place the cemetery is, totally quiet and still, removed from the turmoils of life—floods and accidents, grief and anger, the longing to *know* and understand everything. Yet it doesn't feel empty. It feels peopled with others who have known all these things, felt them and lived them; who would say to her, if they could speak, "It's all right, it all turns out right in the end, no matter what happens. You have to live it as it comes."

A breeze gusts up as she walks, making a swooshing sound in the trees, and red seed pods come whirligiging down. Now she is crying, walking at a slower pace and crying, crying for—what? She doesn't know. Longing for the mother she's never had, loneliness, anger at Shirleen and anxiety for what she might do, confusion about her own future. For Neill's kindness and tenderness that she doesn't want defiled. Gratefulness, too, for the comfort of this old graveyard.

After an hour she leaves and heads towards Logan's store to meet Uncle Frank for a ride home. He comes out as she approaches, and she notices the sag in his shoulders, the tired gesture of his hand as he passes another farmer on the street. He starts up the truck as Norma Jean opens the cab door and climbs in, keeping her head tucked down to hide her puffy eyes. They ride off down the road, silent as usual, Uncle Frank concentrating on his driving.

When they cross the roiling river, Norma Jean looks down and seems to see her own feelings—gushing water, churning and pushing forward against the stanchions of the bridge, splashing and parting around a rock, coming together again with its load of debris—old leaves, half submerged sticks—all of it blasting along with a ferocious roar. Terrifying, exhilarating, beautiful in its wild, tumultuous way, but frightening, out of anyone's control.

"Uncle Frank," she says suddenly, looking up and breaking their silence, "Will you teach me to drive?"

He raises his eyebrows and gives her a faint smile, then pulls into a crossroad where the traffic is sparse.

"We don't have to do it right this minute," Norma Jean says, startled.

"I think we do. You not only have to learn to drive, you have to learn this crazy old truck. You'll get the hang of it, but it'll take a little time. One good thing, there's not much you can do to hurt it."

This first lesson is difficult. The gears whine and squeak as they jerk along. But Uncle Frank seems fine with it, helpful and encouraging. "That's good," he says, "now next time give it a little more gas." Norma Jean marvels at his patience, and the way he seems to be enjoying himself.

***

Although Neill's voice on the phone has become familiar to Norma Jean's household, she's never called his house, and since she's never met his folks, she feels awkward calling there. Her palms are sweaty as she dials his number. "Neill?" says the man's voice on the other end of the line. "Why, yes, I think he's around here somewhere. Who's calling?"

"Oh, it's . . . it's Norma Jean . . . Norma Jean Taylor . . . a friend from Pine Grove."

"Oh, yes, well, all right, let me find him."

Norma Jean breathes a sigh of relief. She has no idea if Neill's even told his parents anything about her. It seems odd when she thinks about it. Aunt Edna likes Neill. She says he seems sensible and polite, not like some. She doesn't know his folks, but she's heard they're "good people." Norma Jean gets the feeling it's a relief to Aunt Edna for her to have a boyfriend at all.

Uncle Frank just likes him. She can tell by the way he rises out of his chair and shakes Neill's hand whenever he comes, how he smiles and asks where they're going, a question she never remembers his asking her.

"Neill, we've got to talk. It's about Shirleen."

"Yeah, I know. Soon as I finish a couple of chores here, I'm pretty sure I can get the car. I'll be over."

***

They drive around some of the rural roads, avoiding Pine Grove, and finally come to an old churchyard shaded with oak trees.

77

"Shirleen called you last night?"

"Yeah, while her folks were at some kind of church supper."

"And what did she say?"

"Well, you know . . ." He laughs. "She asked me to marry her."

"I told her that was a crazy idea. But you can see she's getting desperate. I'm afraid about what she'll do."

"She should have reported that guy right away. Now, *she's* panicking, *we're* worried, and *he* doesn't know or care about any of it."

"Did she tell you I talked to Ethel Posey? She says the *Anna Farraday Home* in Dixon county is a good place, safe and well run, and careful about keeping girls' names private . . . and about who adopts the babies."

"No, she only asked me to take her out to old Essie's place—and help her get the money for it. I'm not going to do it, Norma Jean. I told her I'd think about it and call her back, I will call her back, maybe go over and tell her myself, but nothing about this feels right. Nothing."

"Do you think she'll do something rash? Why is she so set on not telling her parents? I mean, no one would feel good about this, but things happen, you know. And it wasn't her fault. They'll be shocked, of course, but they really love her; they'll take care of her. I've half a mind to go tell them myself."

They sit silently for a few minutes. A gust of wind blows up and stirs the leaves above them.

"Look," Neill says, "here's what I think. We need help. You and me, we can't solve this problem; it's too big for us. I'm going to have a talk with my minister. He's a good guy; he really listens; and he must have helped girls in situations like this before. Anybody else you could talk to?"

Norma Jean looks thoughtful. "Well, not Aunt Edna. She'd march right over there, I know. Not only tell them, but tell them what they better do about it. No, I think . . . I think I'm going to talk to Uncle

Frank. At first I didn't want to, but Shirleen is getting panicky. She said something awful to me the other day. She said my mother went crazy and jumped in the river because she had me." She can feel herself tearing up.

"No one seems to know who my father is, Neill, some stranger my mother was running off with till my grandfather went after them. I should be embarrassed to tell you this, but I'm not. It's just that I know so little about them. What would my life be like if my parents had married, and we'd had a normal family? Or even if my mother hadn't died? What I do know is that my mother was a beautiful young woman, full of life. And I think she loved me. I don't know *why* I think that, but I do."

Tears are flowing now. Neill puts his arms around her and lets her cry. She can feel his cotton shirt getting wet and the strong shoulder beneath it. He pulls out a handkerchief and dabs at her tears. Norma Jean takes it from him to blow her nose.

"I'm sorry," she says. "I didn't mean to get so upset. But it feels good to finally say that to someone."

"Don't be sorry, Norma Jean." He runs his thumb along the side of her face, and looks at her thoughtfully, half smiling, half serious with those green eyes she's come to trust. In the midst of all this turmoil, she suddenly feels safe and unafraid—and something else, too, a warm current of feeling that overrides all the others. He breaks into a wonderful Neill smile and hugs her close.

"Well," he says stepping back, "too bad I have to get the car back. They're strict about that."

"Listen," he says as they drive down the road, "it wouldn't surprise me if lots of folks had to get married. They just try to keep it secret, that's all. There shouldn't be any shame in it." He sighs. "But people talk and some get judgmental about it, say it's bad for community morals and stuff like that. That's so narrow-minded and unfair. It's not your fault."

"No, it's not my fault, but it *is* my family, *my* mother and father. Aunt Edna may mean well. She and Uncle Frank may work hard and take care of all of us. But Julia doesn't belong to her. She's mine—and I have a right to know more about her. I do."

CHAPTER 7

Later that afternoon, Norma Jean paces the attic, her footsteps stirring dust, the old floorboards creaking. What is she asking? Is it so outrageous to want to know about her own mother, to picture her life? Is there anyone in Pine Grove who knows so little about the history of their family? Last night as they sat around the table, she tried again to get Aunt Edna to open up.

"It's interesting to think about this old oak table," she said, "all the people who've sat around it, the stories it could tell. Where did you and my mother sit when you were children, Aunt Edna? Were there cousins your age that came to visit?"

"Long gone and forgotten, Norma Jean." Aunt Edna picked up a serving dish and went to the stove to refill it. "What's the weather look like Frank? Will you be able to plant tomorrow?"

She puts up such a wall against anything connected to their past family. Norma Jean knows she has a grudge against her mother; but after all these years, why is that so strong? Is it jealousy, the way she thought Gram and Travis doted on Julia? Does she blame her for their father's death and Gram's stroke? Or is it all the work that got heaped on her afterwards? Maybe. But as Aunt Edna would say herself, those things are past and done. It seems like there's something more riling her. Norma Jean is puzzled, but she's fed up with her aunt's stony refusal to talk to her about the family. Between that and Uncle Frank's reticence, they're as mute as Gram.

In frustration she turns to the trunks of family clothing, and pictures them hiding inside in their neatly folded layers. "Are you going to let this household silence you forever?" she asks them. Raising her hands in exasperation, she throws up the lid of one close by and tosses up a handful of clothing.

"You were *alive*, weren't you?" she yells and kicks at the trunk. "You farmed; you cooked; you married and had children. Your blood is in my veins"—Norma Jean grabs her wrist and turns the veins toward them like a proof—"your blood and your genes, they're here, *now*, in me. But I know *nothing* of your lives, your looks, even your names." She grabs at the clothes as though she could shake words out of them along with the odor of mothballs and lavender.

Near the dormers, her quilt stands taut on the stretcher, ready for stitching. She wants to seize her largest needle and punch holes into each square, punch till they twitch, till they wake up and look at her, every single one of them, in full attention. The strange sound of her shouting voice echoes in the rafters, before dissipating into silence. Norma Jean slumps to the floor. The weight of the silence exhausts her, her questions no match for its heaviness.

A gray cloud moves from across the sun and the late afternoon light falls through the dusty windows, its slanted rays hitting the quilt full force. As she watches, the colors sharpen vividly and the pattern of each square livens as if at any moment it might start wriggling and shifting in a big splashy commotion. A picture of the churchyard on yearly Reunion Day comes unbidden into her mind. All kinds of folks— young and old, well-dressed and dowdy, sickly and spry—come back to Pine Grove from wherever they've moved, chattering and exclaiming enough to wake their dead ancestors sleeping peacefully and forgotten in the church graveyard. She never knows half of them, but she can often tell by the shape of a nose, a look around the eyes, even the roundedness or angularity of a body, what family would claim them.

Once a large woman in a wide-brimmed hat stared at her, knitting her brows, her lips pursed together. "Who *are* you, child?" she demanded. "I been away a long time, but I can usually see the Pine Grove family in a face." Before Norma Jean could collect herself enough to answer, someone grabbed the woman's arm. "Lottie, Lottie

Baker! How in the world are you?" Norma Jean slipped away through the crowd.

She walked around to the back of the church and sat down on a stump half-hidden behind a big hydrangea bush, the large woman's question echoing in her ears. Who *am* I? she thought. Who am I like? The answers she didn't have pressed on her like stone, and the reunioners milling about nearby were foreigners in a country she would never know.

She feels faint and sits down on the old piano stool in front of the quilt frame. The sun warms her back as though it could melt her into the brightened squares of the quilt. Squinting her eyes, she imagines all the uncles, aunts, and cousins who wore these pieces of material walking around the churchyard, greeting and welcoming each other, hugging, shaking hands, patting children on their heads. As she looks on, the dream scene shifts; it isn't the churchyard where they're congregated; it's the yard around the farmhouse, their home place.

Norma Jean sees herself on one of the lower branches of a peach tree, blossoms blowing and young leaves starting to emerge, watching with delight and fascination as her quilt pieces recreate themselves into the shirts and dresses worn by the crowd. She stares at their faces, at the clothes each is wearing. She notes family resemblances, the vague similarities they share. In a dreamlike way, they feel familiar. Slowly they all move towards the peach tree, looking at her, smiling and nodding their heads. One man with strong shoulders and a weathered face stares at her intently with clear blue eyes and she knows he's her grandfather. They gather around the tree, stray petals floating down among them, and stand at ease smiling up at her in a calm and happy way.

Her heart swells as though it will burst. She sees her grandfather turn his face to the barn, and there in the hayloft doorway, the wind blowing back her dark hair and billowing her white dress, is her mother.

Clouds move again across the sun. Norma Jean blinks and dabs at her eyes. She picks up her needle and, as long as the daylight lasts, sews perfect tiny stitches across the quilt face starting with the square cut from her grandfather's overalls.

***

She lies in her bed that night and thinks about love. How strange it is, how unpredictable. And how it drives people to do things they'd never thought of doing, things that often hurt them or others and lead to disaster. Yet love is supposed to be gentle and caring; that's the message most often heard at church—to love God with all your heart, to love your neighbor as yourself. The first Bible verse she'd ever learned, way back before she could even read, was *God is love*.

At home, sometimes they play music on the radio to soothe Gram if she seems agitated. Once, when she was younger, Norma Jean asked Aunt Edna why so many love songs were sad and lonesome. Aunt Edna was ironing, and she held the iron up and tested its heat with a dab of spit on her finger.

"Just nonsense, Norma Jean, lots of sentimental nonsense. The world never gets enough of it." She pushed the iron down hard on the cuff of Uncle Frank's khaki pants and made a long, sharp crease in the leg. "All these heartache songs just give people an excuse for not getting on with life, not doing the jobs they're supposed to do."

And yet her mother loved her father enough to run off with him, to leave the farm, the only home she'd ever known, and her family, the people who'd always loved her. Grandpa had loved her enough to go after her, to take a gun ready to fight to bring her back. And someone loved her enough to keep a picture hidden in the barn.

Shirleen seems like she *wants* to be in love all the time, so much that she *looks* for boys to fall in love with and does foolhardy, dangerous things to attract them. And she herself already feels something for Neill, something special and different from what she's felt for anyone before. But is this love? She feels no urge to endanger herself, to do something disastrous.

She leaves the bed to sit by her bedroom window opened wide to the night air and stares out into the darkness. Nothing is visible. The familiar farmyard shapes, the barn, the hen house, the grape arbor and peach trees, the fields that run beyond them, the distant line of trees along the river—all hidden in blackness, obscure as the mouth of a cave whose dark passages wind blindly into the unknown.

A deep pang of loneliness runs through her, sharper than she has ever felt. She sees herself sitting on the windowsill of nothingness with no view of past or future. Great tears well up and spill down her face, muffled sobs shake through her body. "I don't understand, I don't understand," she whispers out into the night. Fragments whirl round in her head, vivid and insistent, but refuse to arrange themselves in any order—her whimsical and enchanting young mother, her gypsy father, her rough and solid grandfather lying dead on his own land, the mystery of a faded photograph, the rich colors and textures of the love pocket.

And Shirleen, her flushed excitement over each potential boyfriend, her crumpled, whimpering body among the cedars; the civilized silence that passes for marriage between her aunt and uncle; the warmth of Ethel's closed-in porch where she and Ivy share their lives.

From the pond near the barn a familiar sound breaks through the night, the bellow of bullfrogs voicing their deep courting calls into the amphibian world. She has heard it a thousand times, but never so clearly. The primal nature of their yearning, the insistency of their passion, vibrates through the air and quickens something sharp and indefinable in the pit of her stomach. Two images enter her mind. It would be hard to say which appeared first. One is of her mother looking boldly out of the old photograph in the barn, eager and defiant. The other is Neill, his listening green eyes, his broad smile.

***

Norma Jean waits till there's not a car in sight, then pulls out onto the highway and heads the truck towards town. After a few lessons on country roads she's getting the hang of the gears, how to let out the clutch and push down on the gas pedal before the motor bucks and dies. Sometimes she has trouble finding reverse, and the truck makes an awful grinding sound. But she likes shifting gears, her hand on the knob of the stick, making incremental shifts for more power, and the feel of her foot pumping just enough fuel for the speed.

From time to time Uncle Frank smiles and shakes his head. "Norma Jean, I do believe you've got a feel for it. Lots of folks learn to drive, learn the things you have to do, but you seem to sense it the way some people sense animals. And all this time *I* been driving *you* around."

Norma Jean smiles, too. Each time they go out she's less tense, even looks forward to it. Uncle Frank's a patient teacher, and it's nice, the two of them, having this time together. The cab of the truck is like a little world, a separate space carrying them along.

Another surprising thing is the interest she's taken in how the truck works. She's curious about the way things connect up under the hood, why turning the key makes the motor start, what happens to the water and oil they're forever adding, how the clutch frees the gears. Trying to figure all this out seems like the opposite of making a quilt, more like looking at one already made and puzzling out how the different parts interact to make the whole thing work.

Her questions seem to surprise Uncle Frank, not only because she's a girl, he says, but, as far as he knows, no one else in the family has ever been that mechanical-minded.

"Travis could get things going. He'd tinker and curse at the 'goldarn thing,' and sometimes land a kick or two on a stalled tractor or some other machine. Eventually they'd start up like they didn't dare defy him. But beyond necessity, he wasn't that interested in their workings."

Today they're headed into Pine Grove to try some town driving. Norma Jean is anxious about it. Pine Grove isn't big, but neither are the streets, and what with vehicles going both ways and some parked along the sides, she can already feel the squeeze.

As they cross the river, the old wooden bridge rattles and shakes, and she's grateful they don't meet a vehicle coming the other way. She keeps her eyes glued to the road ahead, no thought of glancing down at the water. They come up behind a wagon loaded with mulch straw and grind along in second gear for the remaining mile into town.

"What if I scrape somebody?" she asks. "Or push on the gas when I mean to brake?"

"Don't worry, everybody goes slow in town. Notice how they'll stop their cars in the middle of the street to say hello to each other? Just watch the clearance on your side of the truck and the rest will be O.K."

Norma Jean's hands are sweating from her grip on the steering wheel; she quickly brushes each one dry against her jeans. They're moving along the main street pretty well until an old man wearing overalls and a straw hat backs a dusty Chevy out of a parking space in front of them. She slams on the brakes, forgetting the clutch altogether, and the truck jumps to a halt.

"Whew," she says, "that was close. Maybe you better take over here, and I'll watch what you do."

"Ed Johnson," Uncle Frank says, shaking his head. "He's got to be at least eighty, and he drives like he's the only car on the road. That was quick stopping. Now start her up again, turn left at Elm, and take us down a few streets."

"Which ones?"

"You decide; you're in the driver's seat."

The neighborhood streets are easy, flat and straight with little traffic, but the turns give her fits—when to gear down, how wide to turn. They jerk and stall and start up again. At one corner when they're at a dead stop in the middle of the street, a black Corvette comes up out of nowhere and honks at them impatiently. Norma Jean floods the engine trying to restart, and the driver pulls around her left side going up on the grass strip between the street and sidewalk and leaving ugly tire marks as he pulls away. Shaken she looks over at Uncle Frank. He shrugs.

"Must be a city fella. Don't worry about it. People do what they do."

They move down Maple Street, and without planning to, Norma Jean turns into the cemetery. Here the narrow road is gravel and one-lane, winding among the markers and family plots.

"Good idea," says Uncle Frank. "Wouldn't have thought of it. No one's going to blindside you here."

They make the full circuit a couple of times, and Norma Jean brings the truck to a halt.

"Mind if we stop a few minutes? It's pretty up here, I'd like to stretch my legs."

They walk slowly in no particular direction. Uncle Frank seems pensive, his hands in the pockets of his green work pants, gazing off towards the fields west of town. Norma Jean knows this is her chance to talk about Shirleen, and she wonders how to start. But inside she feels strangely calm, as though their stroll in this quiet place will go on forever. At one point they pass Julia's grave, and she slows her steps.

"Sometimes I come up here," she says, waving her hand briefly towards the grave. "I don't know why."

He looks at her a moment but doesn't speak, and they walk on. As they approach the truck, Norma Jean stops, takes a deep breath, and turns his way.

"Uncle Frank, there's something I need to talk to you about. I need your advice."

He gives her an anxious look that lets her know he thinks she's going to ask about Julia, so she hurries on.

"A friend of mine's in trouble, big trouble. She wants me to help her, and I want to—but I don't feel right about what she wants me to do."

Norma Jean pauses, hoping he will ask for more details. He leans against the truck with one foot up on the running board, his thumbs hooked in the pockets of his pants, and studies the ground.

"Uncle Frank, it's kind of a life and death matter—or it could be if she does what she's talking about. There's . . . there's a baby involved, you see, and she's in a panic—not thinking straight. I'm worried about what she'll do. She won't tell her parents, and she made me promise I wouldn't tell anyone either, but I think someone should talk to her, reason with her before it's too late. What should I do?"

Norma Jean looks up at her uncle for the first time since she started talking and sees him staring at her, his eyes wide and tired looking, all color drained from his face. She starts to move towards him, but he gives his head a quick shake and turns towards the truck. Placing both hands on the cab, he leans into it and breathes deeply.

"Uncle Frank, are you all right?" she asks with alarm. He nods his head—yes—and takes a few more breaths, then seems to collect himself and straightens up.

"Just a little dizzy spell, caught me off guard. You were talking about your friend, and I. . . ." His face clouds over.

"It's all right, Uncle Frank. We can just go on home if you like."

"Norma Jean, you're asking me for advice, and I hear how upset you are, and worried. I can feel it. Life throws us these things sometimes that we just don't know what to do with. I don't have an answer for you. But I can tell you what I've learned on my own about trying to help other people, people you care about. Sometimes your help isn't wanted. Sometimes it interferes. And sometimes," he sighs, "it leads to more disaster than if you'd stayed out of it altogether. Most times we can't make things turn out the way we want for ourselves, much less somebody else."

Uncle Frank has been looking off in the distance as he talked, but now he faces her straight on.

"So my advice is to let it be. Step back from it, and let whatever happens happen. You can be a steady friend no matter what comes, but it's not yours to fix. That's about all I can say."

He puts his hand on her shoulder in a comforting way and turns to go, but she reaches up and clasps it briefly with her own.

88

"Thank you, Uncle Frank," her eyes are misting. "Thanks for helping me. I'll think on all you've said. It's a side I hadn't thought about. Well," she says, heading towards the truck, "I guess I'm ready to drive us home."

As they turn into Main Street, Norma Jean hears the faint sound of the high school band practicing as they march along on the football field. A few of the older men are sitting in chairs outside the barber shop smoking and swapping stories. Uncle Frank raises a hand in greeting as they pass by. An ordinary day in Pine Grove, just like an ordinary day ten years ago—or ten years to come. For a few minutes, Norma Jean feels the comfort and safety of ordinary life.

CHAPTER 8

She maneuvers the truck up the rutty driveway and pulls it into its usual space by the tool shed. They've been silent for the last part of the ride, and this continues as they open their separate rusty, squeaking doors and step out. Uncle Frank heads for the barn lot, she for the house. After giving Gram a soft hug, she hurries upstairs to the attic, closing the door firmly behind her.

Why is her head feeling so woozy, her heart beating so fast? Let people be, Uncle Frank says, a lesson he learned the hard way. What way? Shirleen's plight seemed to upset him, but his words are helpful. Her own personal feelings *have* gotten mixed up with her wish to help Shirleen.

Not thinking, not crying, numb and lost in a strange space, she sits for a long time on the edge of a trunk, rocking back and forth, her hands clasped together. Her eyes fall on the quilt stretched out on its frame, on the love pocket which seems to beat like a living heart. She rises to touch it, placing her open palm against its center, slowly rotating her hand to feel the textures.

The answer is here, she knows it. From deep inside this pocket of love, vibrations reach out into her own life. But so subtly, like the compelling tones of a whisper whose words are unclear, a message she needs and wants but can't quite hold

Uncle Frank is right, of course. How does *she* know what is best for Shirleen? It's the child that upsets her, the tiny, innocent, helpless baby whose fate will be decided by a frightened and distraught girl. It's herself, her own infant self squirming and flinching in the womb, that she feels bound to protect.

"But you did protect me, Julia." She speaks to the love pocket and feels a sure knowledge that, whatever the circumstances, she was conceived in love.

Somehow Uncle Frank was a part of this. Perhaps Julia was the unspoken love of his life. Perhaps right now he's out in the barn retrieving her picture from the worn billfold. Did he see Julia from the hayloft door that day as she crossed the field in a dress of roses and entered the trees by the river? Was he the one who warned Travis? Norma Jean knows she can never ask him.

She shakes her head, and the tears come streaming down her face. But she is not sobbing. These are grateful tears, tears of awareness, of understanding. How strange, how beautiful and fragile, how very mysterious love is.

***

Norma Jean makes up her mind to be as friendly and available to Shirleen as she can but without trying to tell her what to do. But Shirleen doesn't come to the phone when she calls or answer her notes. She's asked for her seat to be changed to another part of the homeroom and won't even look at Norma Jean in the halls. Though hurt and surprised at being shunned this way, Norma Jean doesn't push it. If this is how Shirleen wants it for now, she'll respect her wishes.

Neill has tried reaching Shirleen, too, and gotten the same rebuff. His minister said he'd be glad to talk to her or her family if Neill felt he could reveal her name, but, other than that, all they can do is pray.

***

Norma Jean stands in the bus line after school and shifts her books from one hip to another. Riding the school bus, closed up with a bunch of rowdy kids, is one thing she will definitely not miss about high school. The sun is warm on her back, but the breeze carries a slight chill. She looks across the street at a row of dusty lilac bushes and is sorry to see the lavender blossoms already starting to fade. Suddenly a car turns the corner and screeches to a stop beneath the shrubs. It takes a moment for her to recognize that it's Neill.

"Don't wait for me, I have a ride," she calls up to the bus driver. As she crosses the street, she's surprised to see him gripping the steering wheel and staring straight ahead.

"Hi," she says, leaning down to the window. "You O.K.?" She can see that he's not. His eyes are troubled, and there's no sign of his usual sunny smile. He looks smaller, too, his shoulders hunched tight.

"Glad I caught you. Can we go somewhere to talk—down to the river maybe?"

As soon as she settles into the passenger seat, he takes off. They drive silently down the road, Norma Jean wondering what's wrong and wishing they were not headed towards those dark familiar waters. Taking a side road that skirts the bank, they stop at a clearing where a wide rock juts out. She'd rather stay in the car, but Neill is already out the door and walking towards the edge. She follows behind and sits down, tucking her skirts around her. The river is running full, glossy in its blackness, and even on this warm afternoon the rock feels cold. She shivers.

"What is it, Neill? What's happened?"

He picks up a stray stick and starts pulling at the bark. "I saw him."

"Who?"

"That guy, the one who raped Shirleen."

"No. Where?"

"In Jackson today. I was coming out of the drugstore after school. He and some of his buddies were there by the curb straddling their big bikes, talking cool and joking. When I walked out the door, I was looking right at him."

"Oh, gosh, I hope Shirleen doesn't see him. No telling what would happen. What did you do? Did you say anything?"

Neill looks down at his hands, slowly twirling the stick, and drops his voice. "No. No," He sighs. "That's just it, I didn't. I didn't say anything. I was shocked to see him; he hasn't been around for months. He's got no idea what Shirleen's been through—probably doesn't even remember her name." He walks to the edge and stares down into the water.

Norma Jean's stomach tightens into a knot. Part of her doesn't want to know this, doesn't want to imagine that this awful person could still be around.

"What was he doing?"

"Just sitting there on his bike, looking so cocky, like the world couldn't touch him." Neill snaps the stick in half and hurls each piece into the water like he's spearing fish. "I wanted to grab him and shake him. I wanted to knock him off that bike and see him groveling in the dust. I've never felt like that before—like I just wanted to beat my fists into someone." His face is red with anger, and his harsh voice startles her. "But I didn't, I didn't."

"Come back from the edge of the rock, Neill. What are you saying?"

He slowly walks back to sit beside her. "I was afraid, Norma Jean. I didn't even tell him about Shirleen. I guess I'm too much a coward." His voice wavers. "I never knew that about myself."

"Oh, Neill," Norma Jean says taking his hands, "you couldn't take on that guy, that whole gang. Even him alone, he's older and bigger and tougher than most of us. I understand you felt you should do something, but you're not a fist fighter. And you're not a coward either."

Neill shakes his head and looks away.

"You always stand up for what you believe is right. I've heard you do it. You're just a different kind of fighter is all. You use your head and your voice. You use your heart." She turns his face towards her. "I think you'll be a lawyer maybe or some kind of advocate helping people who need it. Getting beat up by those guys wouldn't help. You did the right thing."

Neill looks straight at her and squeezes her hands. "You don't understand. I was afraid, Norma Jean. You may be right about different kinds of fighters, but for the first time in my life, I was really scared, paralyzed. I think I understand better how Shirleen feels about the mess she's in. And there's something else I've been afraid about—at least something I've tried to avoid."

Norma Jean is quiet. They can hear the waters tumbling and rushing past them. Here they are, talking about fear beside the Black River that she has been afraid of all her life, afraid of what it did to her mother, afraid for her unborn self, afraid to move any direction for fear of where she herself will end up.

"Norma Jean, my folks, they haven't wanted me to see you. They're just, well, real puritanical in their religion, you see. I guess they can't help it; it's the way they were raised. But they remember the tragedy, the whole business about your granddad and mother." A flush crosses his face as he looks down. "They keep telling me about 'nice girls' in Jackson I should take an interest in."

She's never thought of herself as anything but an ordinary "nice girl."

Neill hurries on. "I've just sort of ignored their whole attitude, it's so far off base. But I'm not going to do that anymore. I'm going to tell them tonight how wrong they are, what a special, thoughtful girl you are and how friendly your family has been to me. I think they'll come round, and I *know* they'll think you're special, too, when they meet you."

Norma Jean shakes her head slowly from side to side, then reaches out for Neill's hand. "It took courage for you to tell me that, Neill. You're very special to me, too." With a smile of relief and tenderness, he takes her face in his hands and kisses her. When he pulls away, they both smile, then laugh out loud.

You know," she says slowly, "what I just said to you about being a different kind of fighter in whatever work you do—it's funny, I just realized, just now, what I want to do. I want to work with babies that need a good home, help them somehow to find the right place where people will really care for them and love them. They're the ones I most want to help."

Neill looks puzzled. "You do? How?"

"I don't know exactly. I don't know what training I'd need or who to ask. Who could I talk to?"

"Gee, I don't know either. Maybe the director of the place you told Shirleen about."

"Yeah, maybe I could. I'll think about it some more, but you know what?—I'm starting to feel excited just thinking about it."

Norma Jean rises and tugs at his hand. "Come on, Neill, let's get going."

***

April is finally here. Though it's a slow spring, rainy and some days are cool, the birds are singing and darting about cheerily, busy with their nest-building. Ella Mae is pleased to announce the sale of Minnie Lewis' quilt in Jackson for $60, of which she will get $45. And the store owner is asking for more.

"My word!" exclaims Bea. "What was the name of that shop? I may start quilting for profit!"

"Do you think we're becoming fashionable?" asks Ethel with a laugh. "Maybe I should buy a new hat!"

Norma Jean smiles, too. "I *am* seeing more and more quilted clothes in the magazines at Logan's—patchwork skirts and vests and such. It's funny how styles get started."

"Well, times change," says Ella Mae. "And that leads me to something I want to bring up. Minnie is looking for a regular place to quilt. Her house is small and her grandchildren so boisterous, she has trouble finding the time and space to do that kind of work at home. What would you think about inviting her to join us? You've already seen an example of her talent."

No one says anything for a few minutes, startled by Miss Ella Mae's suggestion.

"You mean *here*, in the church?" Bea asks. "Oh, I don't think they'd allow it. And Charlie wouldn't allow me to come. You know, 'separate, but equal.' That's how it's supposed to be. We don't want to stir up trouble."

"Well," Norma Jean says, "I'd like it. I think we could learn things from watching how she quilts. I've waited on her in the store; she's a warm and polite person."

"Let's just think about it for now," Ella Mae says. "Mull it over and we'll talk about it again."

***

"Uncle Frank, how did you know what you wanted to do? Did you always know you would farm?"

They are driving cross-county to look at a cow Uncle Frank's thinking of buying. The wooden sides are up on the truck bed in case they decide to bring her home, and Norma Jean is to drive back so he can keep an eye on things through the rear window.

"Huh," he says, shaking his head, "that's a question never occurred to me, what I wanted to do. Most of us back then, we just did what was there without thinking about it. What I mean is, it weren't like we had a choice."

"Oh." Norma Jean tries to imagine what that would be like, to have no choice, have only one way open to you, to know most all your life what you would always be doing. "That sounds . . . well, hard. Like you might end up doing what was all wrong for you, something you hated even."

"Yep, some folks did, I'm sure. But mostly people didn't think like that. They did what they did, and if they did O.K., made enough to live on and raise their families, they were satisfied."

They're on a gravel road now, ten or twelve miles from home, rocks crunching under their tires and rutted spots bouncing them around. They pass a country store, and a little further on, Mt. Hebron, one of two colored churches in the county, flanked by tall poplar trees and an old graveyard. Cars and pick-up trucks are parked near the building.

"Must be a funeral," says Uncle Frank, "all those folks out here on a week day—such a hot one, too." He lifts up his straw hat in respect as they pass and looks down at the dashboard.

"She's heating up under the hood. Guess we better stop at the next group of shade trees we find and give her a rest. I'll put more water in the radiator once she cools off."

Trees are few on these roads between the fields, but they see a farmyard ahead and pull in under a couple of maples. No one seems to be around, probably out in the fields, but Uncle Frank knows the farmer and says he won't mind. They climb out, leaving the doors open, and he raises the hood. Norma Jean leans against a tree and thinks about having no choice in your life versus the pressure of having to choose. She wonders which is hardest.

He seems to be reading her mind when he says, "You know, it's like this gravel road—noisy and bumpy compared to macadam, but before it was graveled, it was just dirt, one lane with ruts and washouts, and people were glad to have it because before *that* there was only wagon tracks or you just made your way alongside the fields. Nowadays you get to choose which paved road you want to follow. I don't know

96

what I'd a done with that. I was lucky to have any road at all." Sprinkling tobacco on a cigarette paper, he rolls it up and seals it.

Norma Jean stares at him in amazement. It's the most words she can remember him volunteering at one time, and it makes her realize how little she really knows him—as Frank Johnson, that is, the boy, the young man, the man standing before her, and not just as her uncle.

"What was it like when you were growing up, Uncle Frank? I mean I know your mom and dad have been gone a long time, that he farmed, too. But . . . how was it?"

Uncle Frank shrugs. "Again, it was what it was. We were sharecroppers down in this part of the county. Ma died when I was just a little 'un. Pa farmed his share and had me out in the fields young as I can remember. It took both of us, and we still didn't have enough. When I was fourteen, he pulled me from school and hired me out to the land-owning farmers for as much as he could spare me. That's how I met Edna, you know, working for Travis, though he was Mr. Taylor to me then. Never dreamed I'd be running the place one day."

"So not having a choice worked out for you? I mean, you wanted to keep on farming?"

"Yes, I suppose I did. I'm at home on a farm with the crops and the animals. I guess you'd have to say, in that way at least, it worked out." He finished filling the radiator and slammed down the hood. "Let's move on."

She wonders what he means by "*that way at least*." She knows enough about farm life to know that going from a sharecropper to a landowner, while not unheard of, is not common either. In fact, it's a big step. You could usually pick out the sharecropper kids in school. Some looked dirty, like the dust was part of their skin. They had funny, chopped off haircuts unless their heads had been shaved for ringworm. Their noses were always running, and they brought bread and butter sandwiches for lunch. By the time they were ready for high school, a lot of them dropped out to work in the fields or ran away to some city or even got married and started their own brood.

Still, if you didn't *have* a choice, you wouldn't have to blame yourself if things didn't work out. Choosing up front what you'll do is scary, though everyone seems to expect you to do it.

"We'll be at the Hobbs place, soon," says Uncle Frank. "A couple of miles more. But since you asked, I'm gonna show you something." They turn down a lane marked Jeffords Road. Here and there, on either side, small cabins appear—washed red with faded paint or covered with random pieces of siding. The roofs are tin and gleam in the sun except for the part shaded by a single tree, usually with an old tire hanging from a limb as a swing.

"Over there." Uncle Frank points to one near a thicket of trees grown up along a little stream. "That was our cabin. Wondered if I'd find it standing. Pa ran a still back in those woods. Brought in some cash and gave him a free supply. I think Mr. Jeffords knew it, but he let it be. Maybe he got his share of that, too." He pauses for a minute. "Edna's never seen this place, never asked to. Course she knew we sharecropped on Jeffords farm, guess that was enough. But she sure don't know about the still, so don't mention it." He smiles slightly and turns to face her. "Don't know why I'm showing you, except you was asking, and we was near."

He turns the truck around and takes a last look towards the little shack. "Guess I just wanted someone to know where I come from."

Norma Jean is quiet, moved by the closeness she feels to him at that moment in the cab of the truck.

"Thanks, Uncle Frank," she says softly. "Thanks for showing me."

***

The Hobbs place is mainly a cattle farm. Instead of field after field of crops, there are large stretches of grassland, more rolling than their part of the county, with a few rock outcroppings and a winding stream passing through. They pass a sizable herd on their way to the barn, and Norma Jean is pleased to see a few young calves nursing or standing close to their mothers. When they stop the truck in the barnyard, however, a distressing sound reaches her ears, a raw, bleating sort of call that repeats itself again and again in melancholy echoes.

"What's that?" she asks, looking towards the barn for explanation.

"That'd be the calves," says Uncle Frank, "the ones they separated out from their mothers."

"Oh my, must be a lot of them. They sound so sad, so frightened. It hurts me to hear them cry like that. Why must they do it?"

"Well," Uncle Frank shrugs, "it does sound awful to hear them bawl. Like weaning a baby, they don't like it. But they'll get over it in a few days once they take to the corn mash and such."

"Won't they still want their mamas?"

"Guess not if they quit bawling. Like most animals, I doubt they'll remember—not this young."

The sound intensifies, like a longing in the deepest part of their bellies. Norma Jean thinks Uncle Frank must be wrong about the calves. You couldn't feel anything that strongly and forget.

"Come on," says Uncle Frank, walking towards the barn "let's go look at this heifer. There's nothing to be done about the calves."

"But will they just become part of the herd?" she says catching up with him.

"Well," he pauses "this is a business, you know. This time of year, a lot of them go off to market."

***

Norma Jean lies in bed hearing the calves' bewildered cry in her head. She wonders if human babies, separated from their mothers and put up for adoption feel the same distress. How could they not? She felt the calves' pain as if it was her own. Perhaps it was, a long ago wrenching away that had never healed.

99

She thinks about secrets: Uncle Frank's pa and his still in the woods; secret hiding places like the old wallet she'd found hidden in the barn; secret meeting places like the smooth little sandbar on the Black River; the secret story of her mother's death and of her own life, her secret father. And now Shirleen's terrible secret, causing such anguish.

There's even her own secret, the quilt she's putting together from the cut up pieces of family clothing. Although she wants desperately to know the locked-up secrets of her family, about her quilt she feels very private. It's special to *her*, something she needs to withhold till she's ready to show it. Is she protecting herself from questions and comments that might be distracting, make her doubt what she's doing? And is something even a secret, if nobody wants to know it?

Shirleen is protecting *herself* from shame and judgment, maybe protecting her parents, too. But not her baby. The baby seems a threat to her safe life, to the way she wants to live it. Who are Aunt Edna and Uncle Frank protecting? They say it's Gram, but she wonders. Could it be themselves—or each other? Even Norma Jean or those who can no longer speak?

Maybe this is true of all secrets—that they come from fear of one kind or another, that people hold back information to keep themselves safe or those they love. Her mother, not much older than Shirleen now, had chosen to keep *her*, to give her life, but she'd also kept secret her father's name and the events of her grandfather's death. *I don't want to know their deepest secrets*, thinks Norma Jean. *I just want to know about my mother, what she was like and why she died. I just want to keep her alive in me.*

***

Norma Jean is halfway down the steps when she stops to listen. It takes her a few minutes to make out the sound she hears coming from the back of the house. Is it laughter? She had left Neill on the front porch while she went up to get her sweater. He must have wandered back to the kitchen where Aunt Edna is making pineapple upside-down cakes for the church bake sale.

100

Surprised and curious, she walks slowly down the hall and stops at the kitchen door. Aunt Edna, her face red and perspiring, is wiping tears from her eyes with the bottom of her apron.

Norma Jean stands in the doorway, perplexed and feeling awkward, not quite sure what to do. They are too busy laughing to even see her.

"What's funny?" she asks.

Aunt Edna wipes her glasses and starts to speak. "Well, I was— I was just telling Neill that . . . and he . . ." She doubles over again in laughter.

Neill, leaning back against the sink, hands braced on the gray porcelain, is grinning widely and shaking his head. Norma Jean is stiff and expressionless. She's never heard laughter in the house before, not like this. It makes her uncomfortable and feeling left out of the joke. When they don't answer, her irritation rises.

"Well," she says, "call me when you can talk," and turns from the room.

"Hey," says Neill, "don't leave. We just got tickled because—"

Norma Jean heads out the front door, letting the screen slam behind her. She almost trips on the top step, catches herself on the railing, then walks briskly in the direction of the peach trees. Losing herself in their flurry of blossoms, she grabs a low branch with both hands and leans her weight into it. The door slams again. Looking up, she sees Neill stop for a moment, then leap down the steps and head in her direction. She turns her head back away from the house.

"Hey," he says, "what happened? You O.K.?"

She doesn't answer.

"Norma Jean, don't be mad. We didn't mean to ignore you. It was just—-you know how it is when you start laughing about something and can't stop."

"No," she says rubbing her toe in the ground beneath the tree. "No, I don't know, Neill." She looks off through the blossoms towards the greening fields. "And I don't *know* why I'm upset. It's just that"— she turns towards him, rubbing the red imprint of the bark on her hands—"Aunt Edna never laughs like that. I've never seen her so— she's always working and busy, she hardly ever even talks to anyone unless she's telling them what to do. And to see her so different, so relaxed . . ."

Norma Jean looks up at Neill, surprised to feel her eyes misting up. "You know, we never laugh in this house. It just hit me that no one laughs here, not big laughs like that one."

Neill wipes away a tear with his finger. "Is that right? Well, that *is* sad. My folks are serious about work and being a good citizen and stuff, but I guess we laugh a lot, especially at my goofy little brother, the way he gets his words mixed up and says funny things."

"They say my mother was a happy person, she must have laughed a lot. But I guess things got real serious in my family about the time I was born."

"Yeah, well, from all you've told me happened, I can understand that. But, hey," he says, taking her hands, "you know what? You don't have to stay that way. You can . . . lighten up, find your funny bone?" He bends her arm and rubs her elbow in his palm.

In spite of herself, Norma Jean smiles. "Well, maybe, but people can't change the way they are—just like that."

"Right. This will have to be gradual, a slow shift in outlook. Laughter Education 101. Now, Miss Taylor," His expression becomes serious and scholarly, "can you tell me one humorous thing you've noticed in the past week? Just one."

His professor mimic is so funny, Norma Jean laughs in spite of herself. "You, you are the funniest boy I know."

He rubs his chin. "Hm, I'm not sure we can credit that answer— but it's a start. Now, your assignment is—to laugh twice, right in this house, before the next class.

"But what if nothing's funny?"

"Everything has its funny side; it's just that the serious can overwhelm it. How about Shirleen asking me to marry her? Now, who in your house sometimes has an expression that looks just like a bullfrog?"

Norma Jean laughs out loud. She's seen that expression dozens of times—Aunt Edna's bulging eyes when she's being very serious.

***

Norma Jean and Neill move along Hwy. 8 and cross the line into Dixon County. The Anna Farraday Home is still a good fifteen miles away, over near Jasper, and she sees the subtle change in terrain from flat farmland to hills and valleys.

"I wonder how old she is," Norma Jean says. She has written to Miss Timberlake, the director, stating her concern for unwanted babies and asking for an appointment. The response was friendly but formal, suggesting a time the following week. Norma Jean is clear that this visit is just to get information, not a job interview or anything, but she hasn't told Aunt Edna where she's going or even about her new idea. She wants to have her own thoughts sorted out before she opens the subject to her aunt's scrutiny.

"That's a good question," Neill says and shrugs. "I wonder how old a person would be to have a job like this. It'd be interesting to find out how she ever got into this work herself."

They find the place a couple of miles outside of town but almost pass it by. Set back a bit from the road, it looks like any country house, white with a wraparound porch and several oak trees in the yard. The small sign on the gate just says *Anna Farraday Home*, nothing about unwed mothers. There's even an old hound dog that saunters out to meet them as they come up the gravel drive.

Neill plans to wait in the car to avoid embarrassing any of the young girls, but Norma Jean feels self-conscious herself as she mounts the steps to the porch. Two girls, pretty far into their time, are sitting in rockers shelling lima beans; they give her a curious look, and she

103

realizes, with a start, they are assessing her as a new resident. Norma Jean colors, says a faint "hello," and opens the screen door.

The hallway inside is polished and cool, a breezeway between the front and back doors. A sizable parlor is on the left, a dining room on the right, but no one in sight. She hesitates, wondering what to do, when a door opens further down the hall and a brisk little lady wearing a navy skirt, white shirtwaist blouse and sensible shoes comes forward to meet her. Her hair is dark, but graying, cut simply and short, and glasses on a beaded chain hang down from her neck.

"Miss Taylor," she says, extending her hand. "I've looked forward to meeting you. Come back to my office and let's get acquainted."

Norma Jean pauses. She has never shaken hands with a woman before, and it takes her a moment to realize what's expected. But the hand that clasps hers is warm and reassuring. If she herself were here of necessity, this would be a good hand to shake.

They settle into a small room that has a desk, two wooden chairs, and a round braided rug. But what Norma Jean sees first are the pictures of babies that cover the walls. Snapshots of all kinds of infants: bald, fair-haired, heads covered with dark ringlets; fat cheeked or narrow-faced like wizened old men, scowling or yawning or looking startled by the camera. She's never imagined so many kinds of babies, has always considered them pretty much alike for the first year.

"So you like my gallery," Miss Timberlake says. "That's a good sign for someone who is thinking about working with infants. Most of the young women part with their babies soon after they are born and never see them again. But they know these pictures are always here, a reminder of the birth they have given and the gift they have bestowed on some childless couple or family. I think it helps their spirits during these waiting days."

A gift they will bestow. The words echo in Norma Jean's head. She has never thought of unwed mothering as anything but sad and shameful and tragic. Is it possible to imagine that she and Shirleen's baby and others like them could be a gift?

They talk for an hour or more, Miss Timberlake describing her training and work experience, the rewards and challenges of the job. Norma Jean feels a growing excitement and is surprised to find herself talking more than usual, asking questions, expressing concerns, bringing up problems such as the money she'd need to get any training. The director listens with interest and smiles encouragement.

"You know, I talk to many young women, Norma Jean. Perhaps it's insight gained from the work that enables me to help them as much as it is my training. And my insight today tells me that you are headed in the right direction." She smiles broadly. "We'll find you the training somehow. There's a great need for more people in this field. I'll start writing letters to those I know. We may discover an internship for you, too, if nothing else appears right away—probably with babies at first rather than a home like this one. You're too near the age of these girls. They might envy your freedom to choose being here and feel you too innocent to relate to their situation."

"Miss Timberlake, this seems like such a good and hopeful place for girls who find themselves in trouble. But why don't more of them know about places like Anna Farraday? For some, the first thing they think of is how to get rid of the baby. That seems so sad and dangerous to me—for everyone involved."

"Yes, that's true. Unfortunately, often they're so panicked and ashamed, they just want to solve the problem as quickly as possible, pretend it never happened. I worry about them, the effect it will have on *their* lives later on. Of course, there are good midwives out there, always have been, and in a strange way, we are working together. I dream of the day when a young woman in trouble can go to one place and get good counseling that will help her make her own choice. But none of it's legal yet; our society's just not ready for it."

Miss Timberlake rises as a bell rings the noon hour. "You'll hear from me soon, my dear. But you must go home and talk to your aunt and uncle. They will need to support you in whatever develops." She holds out her hand in goodbye. This time Norma Jean grasps it with a new fervor, unaware of her feet on the floor, she opens the screen door to a new world, one of vision and purpose. She's so elated she barely notices that the two young women are gone.

Down the drive she sees Neill parked under a tree, doubtless reading the book he's brought, and she's about to run out to him when something catches her eye, a figure in the far right side of the yard, sitting on a faded glider and mindlessly pushing it back and forth.

Against her usual inclination, Norma Jean takes a few steps in that direction, hesitates, stares at the occupant who is facing the other way, then walks slowly forward.

"Shirleen," she says softly. The swinging stops and the girl sits frozen for a minute, then slowly turns her head.

"What are *you* doing here?" Shirleen demands. "Was it you who went to my parents, told them to call the doctor?"

"What? No. Did they find out? Is that why you're here.?"

"*Is that why I'm here?*" mocks Shirleen. "Why else would I be? That doesn't explain why you're here. Did they send you to check up on me?"

"Shirleen," Norma Jean moves around in front of her. "I didn't know *what* you were doing. And, no, I haven't told anyone. I thought about it, I confess I did. But just because I was worried what you'd do. You made it clear you didn't want to see me, so I've just stayed away."

Shirleen looks down at her lap, and Norma Jean can see she believes her. "Oh, Shirleen," she says, taking a seat on the glider and grasping her balled up fists, "I'm so glad to see you here. I was so afraid you'd gone to that . . . woman, that you and the baby might both be harmed."

Shirleen pulls in her breath and expels it with sobs that come one after the other. She leans into Norma Jeans arms and allows her to pat her back and stroke her hair. Just like you would a baby, Norma Jean thinks.

"I tried to go, Norma Jean. I got almost enough money together, taking a little bit here and there from Daddy's billfold. And I know where Mama hides her hard-times cash. I started out there, too, sneaked out after they were both in bed. Clara Chumley took me. But I couldn't do it. I couldn't go through with it. I was too afraid—that road through the woods, that rough little cabin. I didn't even go up the steps, just ran back to Clara's car and crept back in the house so sick and tired I couldn't leave my bed. The third day, Dr. Marsh walked in—right into my room. I guess they'd called him 'cause I hadn't seemed right. Mama is always such a worrywart. He examined me and told them. Such carrying on. I explained how it happened, but really I was too tired of it to care. Dr. Marsh worked it out to come here. I came last week."

Norma Jean smiles and shakes her head. "I knew you weren't in school, but I had no idea you were here. I came out to talk to Miss Timberlake about doing a job like hers. And she's going to help me figure out how. She's a good person, Shirleen. Give her a chance, I think she'll be a friend to you. Your folks'll get over it. They love you too much not to."

"Yeah, I know they do. But maybe that's been part of the problem. It's kind of suffocating, like I had to really push against them to get some air on my own. Anyway, I'm glad that when this—she looks down at her bulging body—is all over, they're sending me to my aunt's in Ohio. I'm ready to get out of Pine Grove."

"I've been having the same thoughts, Shirleen. It's time to move forward, step out into my future." Norma Jean feels her eyes misting up. "Let's promise to write each other, to really keep in touch about how it's going, what's happening, both the good and the troublesome—and the questions we have. Will you do that, Shirleen? You've always been my closest friend here in Pine Grove."

"Oh, yes. I want to do that. You've been my best friend, too, Norma Jean." The apology she had hoped to hear for the harsh words about her mother doesn't come. Still, the girls embrace, each giving and receiving a long hug. Wiping tears from her cheeks, Norma Jean walks away, wondering when and how they will ever see each other again.

CHAPTER 9

Norma Jean pulls out of the driveway onto the blacktop and heads away from town. Uncle Frank wants her to practice driving by herself on some of the county roads where there's little traffic, just a farm truck every now and then or a tractor moving from field to field west of the river. She's familiar with most roads nearby, but none of them are marked so she keeps track in her head—going past the Turner farm, turning left at the crossroads, passing the old lumber mill, taking the right fork at Bryce's store.

She'd been nervous about setting out alone, but she starts to enjoy it. Fields stretch out on either side, the sky spreads blue above, and except for a distant farmer or two and a few clumps of cattle, she might be the only living person in the world. The truck kicks up dust behind her, an orange cloud covering her tracks, screening her from where she's been.

She smiles to herself and whistles a nameless tune as the truck jostles along. Her eyes narrow. Up ahead there's something to the left, between the road and the big drainage ditch that runs along a cornfield. As she gets closer, it becomes a person, small like a child, but not moving or waving her to stop. She slows the truck and hesitates. An old colored woman sits on the edge of the ditch, watching the truck with an expressionless face. An unaccountable chill slides through Norma Jean's body. She wants to keep going like she hasn't seen anyone, but it's lonely out here, maybe she's hurt.

She slows to a stop a few yards after passing her. The woman doesn't move. Norma Jean gets out of the truck and walks towards her. Though she looks old, her spare body is what Uncle Frank would call "tightly coiled." The dark skin is pulled tight across her forehead and cheekbones. Her short wiry hair is held back by what looks like the sash of an old dress wrapped double around her head. Ropey veins stand out in her neck. Even sitting on the ground, Norma Jean can see she's short, much shorter than herself, more like the size she'd been at twelve. But something about her is big, alert as a bobcat, even though one foot lies twisted and bare, its laceless shoe resting halfway down the rough bank.

"Who you is?" the woman asks abruptly. "I know you?"

Norma Jean steps back. The strong voice startles her and the sharp, appraising look seems to figure her out before she can think what to answer.

"I . . . you're hurt, aren't you? Can I . . . can I get somebody? Take you to someone?"

The woman sits unmoving, studying her face. Norma Jean feels the sweat breaking out on her brow.

"You scared of me, ain't you?" The woman raises her chin as though she's looking down at Norma Jean, even from her seat on the ground. "Why you white girls always so scared? Scared of black folks, old folks, dead folks—sometime seem like you scared to be living. Fetch me that shoe there, missy."

Norma Jean scrambles down the bank to get it, shaking out dust and pebbles before handing it over. Who is this wizened little woman sitting in the dirt like a queen?

"Give me your hand, girl. Help me get righted up."

Norma Jean grasps her palm and elbow to raise her. The woman slips her foot into the shoe and tries taking a step. It's no good. The ankle's been twisted somehow and won't hold her.

"I got to get home, girl. Can you tote me in the back of your truck?"

"But . . . shouldn't you see a doctor?"

"Ha—me see a doctor. That's a good one. Ain't no doctor knows better what to do than me. Besides, things heal theirself if you gives 'em time, if you knows how to help 'em along." She reaches inside the front of her dress and pulls out a rabbit's foot hanging from an old string round her neck. Next to it is a tiny bag, red but faded with age and bulging with whatever it holds inside. When she sees Norma looking at it, she holds up the rabbit's foot and chuckles.

"This rabbit foot ain't help *my* foot today, has he? Yes, ma'm, that's the way it seem. But you don't know, missy, you don't know. That fall might've save me from stepping on old mister cottonmouth. Or might be I's suppose to be sitting here by this road waiting for you. Come on now." She spits tobacco juice towards the ditch and gestures impatiently at the truck.

"Maybe I should go get Uncle Frank. I mean, it's his truck, he'll know better what to do."

The woman looks at Norma Jean quizzically. "Who your folks, child? Uncle Frank who?"

Norma Jean's hands get sweaty, her throat dry. A simple question, but she hesitates to answer.

"I, uh, Uncle Frank, he's my uncle. I mean, I live with him and Aunt Edna . . . back there . . . off Black River Road. The Taylor place."

"Um, hmm, I should've knowed." The woman nods her head with a tight-lipped smile. She looks Norma Jean in the eye. "You Miss Julia's baby then, her baby girl, 'most grown now—what? seventeen, eighteen years there about?"

Norma Jean stares back at her, speechless. A flutter of excitement mixes with wariness in her stomach. In all her years of asking, no one's ever volunteered to mention her mother's name.

"You knew her?" she asks, dumbfounded.

The black woman chuckles, then spits again making a small brown puddle in the dust. "Course I knowed her. Miss Julia weren't one to sit home. She wander all over the place. Yes . . ." her gaze shifts away, "I know that girl. Course," she turns back, eyeing Norma Jean, "I knows lots of folks hereabouts. It's my business to know. Come on now . . ." She nudges Norma Jean who helps her step forward on her good foot.

"What your name?"

"It's . . . Norma Jean."

"Awright, Miss Norma Jean, grab hold. Let's get off this hot road and put old Essie in the truck."

Essie! Norma Jean blanches. Is this Essie, the old woman Shirleen talked about, the one who lives back in the woods? She looks up and down the road—no one in sight, no clouds of dust to show anyone coming. She helps her hobble to the back of the truck, not sure what she's doing or why. This woman knew her mother. She needs help. But she's strange, so strange, and if she does what Shirleen says . . .

"Put the gate down, miss. It ain't far. I'll ride on the edge so my feets can dangle. Just go easy on them bumps."

Essie leans back on the tailgate and Norma Jean locks her hands together, works them under the shoe of Essie's good foot and hoists her up. It's a man's shoe, worn and dusty, and the weight of it in her palms feels rough and solid.

She climbs into the cab of the truck and stares at the key in the ignition. Holding on to the steering wheel she takes a deep breath. Her heart races so fast, she wonders if she can drive. The directions are clear enough—go on down the road and over the little bridge that crosses Johns creek. Take a left onto the dirt road beyond, then a right at the first lane into the woods . . . into the woods. Norma Jean shivers, half afraid, half excited. Suddenly she feels far from home, from the snug comfort of her attic. Can she trust this shriveled old woman? Will she tell her the truth? What if Aunt Edna's right—that there're things better *not* to know?

She looks through the back window in time to see Essie spit another shot of tobacco juice. The old woman sits straight-backed on the tail of the truck, her head erect on her small, boney frame. Norma Jean takes hold of the key and turns it. For once the engine catches on the first try.

She drives slowly down the center of the road, aware of the loose gravel crunching beneath the wheels. Every now and then she glances into the rearview mirror and each time sees the same dark figure sitting as straight as Aunt Edna in church. In about half a mile they cross Johns

111

creek. Norma Jean slows to a stop at the narrow dirt road on her left. It stretches out flat as a ribbon, but it's lower than the main road, the downhill grade could roll her passenger forward on the truck bed. She looks into the back and sees Essie waving her on.

Shifting into first gear, she eases the vehicle down the bank and flattens off. The road ahead looks ridged and bumpy. In the past, Norma Jean's seen bushels of corn and bales of hay bounce around on better roads than this, and she remembers how she and Shirleen had fun as kids bumping across the farm in the back of the truck when Uncle Frank went out to inspect the fields. They would roll around, fall against each other, bumpity-bump along, shrieking and giggling the whole time. But a woman with a hurt ankle, sitting on the tailgate?

Yet it seems this old woman has little regard for mishap. Besides, Norma Jean's had plenty of experience on their own rutty driveway. At least the road is dry, she can see how to maneuver.

The lane they turn into disappears in the pine needles that cover the ground. Trees are tall and thick here, making deep shade even in the heat of day. Norma Jean thinks of the bats and owls and snakes that must fill these woods at night. She follows the only clear way ahead making turns right or left when trees block her way. The wheels are quiet on the soft needles except for the snap of dry sticks or the crunch of pine cones beneath them. In spite of its strangeness, there's a comfort about this place—the coolness, the smell of pine, the breeze soughing through the upper branches. Breathing in the air calms her, her fingers loosen on the wheel, and her curiosity stirs about her passenger.

She follows the lane around another turn, and there it is—an old weathered cabin. Two dogs jump off the porch and run barking and snarling up to the truck. They have eyes like wolves and short thick tails. Essie slaps the side of the truck with her hand, and they run towards her, making whining sounds in their throats.

Norma Jean cautiously opens the door as Essie calms the dogs, speaking words she can't make out. They trot off to the porch and pay her no mind. She helps Essie down from the truck bed, then over to the house. Even with a limp, Norma Jean feels the strength in her taut body.

112

Rusting tin cans line the porch, different sizes holding plants that look healthy and well-tended. Most are unfamiliar, but she recognizes mint and heal-all. The cabin sits in the midst of a clearing, sun streaming down toward the porch creating a well of light in the dark woods.

Essie motions toward an old cane chair on the porch, and Norma Jean lowers her into the seat. "Draw us some water, girl," she says, nodding towards a pump at the far end. A bucket sits on the porch's edge nearby, a metal dipper resting inside. Norma Jean's used to pumping for the cow trough at their barn, and she's glad to have a task. She gets the water spurting in a couple of motions and notices how dry her own mouth feels. The water is cool, refreshing.

Essie takes a long, slow draft from the dipperful Norma Jean hands her. Her eyes look fixed and trancelike, as if she's deep inside herself. Norma Jean settles down on the top step and stares off into the woods.

"You wanting to know things 'bout your ma, ain't you?"

Norma Jean reddens and nods her head.

"Essie don't spread talk, don't give out stories. If she did, wouldn't nobody come. For sure she don't rankle the dead."

Norma Jean looks down and nods her head.

"You a different case, I think. I'm getting a feeling, a voice speaking to me. Wants you to know some things. But just you, nobody else. It wants to know can you promise that, can you swear to it?"

Looking Essie in the eye, Norma Jean nods again.

"I knowed Miss Julia. She used to pass by here, ask 'bout my herbs. She knew what to ask. The dogs, they never bark at her neither. They knowed a spirit-walker when they seen one."

Spirit-walker. Norma Jean's never heard of that. But it feels right. "People say she was different . . ."

"She different all right," says Essie. "She had the gift . . . could see things, hear things. And she follow what she hear. But she be young, folks talk. Easier to be an old woman living out in the woods; everybody think you crazy anyway and don't pay you no mind."

There's a question Norma Jean has to ask, something she must know. "Did she . . . before I was born, did she . . . want to have me?"

Essie shifts the tobacco plug to the other side of her mouth and looks deep at Norma Jean. "You mean did she want me to help her get rid of you? No indeed, missy, no indeed. Some girls do, they needs to do that. But that the last thing on Miss Julia's mind. She knowed you was meant to be born. I knowed it, too, knowed she was having you even before she did. I birthed you, you know."

Norma Jean's mouth drops open.

"Yes ma'am, I was there. I birth lots of babies round here, most all the colored ones—white ones, too, when that doctor from Jackson ain't around. Or folks wants to keep things quiet. You came out easy. She smile when she saw you."

Norma Jean feels a heaviness lifting from her, her body so full of light, she might rise right up in the air. She can see her young mother and Essie and her baby self, like it was happening right before her.

"I wish she was still here. I wish I could know her."

"You knows her. You knows her better than most folks who *was* there. Some people be too alive for others to touch, like they 'fraid they get burned."

Essie looks hard at Norma Jean, then out into the trees. "You go on home now. I don't 'spect to see you here no more."

"But . . . I might want to ask . . ."

"Whatever answers you need, you'll get without asking me. It ain't fitting, young girl like you be hanging 'round here. You like your mama some ways, I can see. But some ways you different. You need to mind that, mind it good."

"One more question, Essie, just one. Do you know who my father was?"

"No, I don't. Weren't none of my business to know. But I know it weren't Mr. Frank. He just love her."

***

Norma Jean drives away in a daze. When she finds herself at the junction of Black River Road, she has no memory of driving there, as though a magic carpet had sailed her along over ruts and gravel and crossroads. "Head in the clouds" Aunt Edna would say. She probably shouldn't be driving. But she's not ready to go home. Above all, she doesn't want to talk to anyone.

She turns right and drives towards Jackson. Here she is, moving down this road, just like Julia did, seeing the same fields and barns and silos *she* saw, feeling the same air in her face, smelling the same plowed earth. *I'm like her.* The magic of those words repeats like a charm—*I'm like her, I'm like her.* It's almost too much to contain. But the other voice, the one that says she's *different*, is there, too, like a deep bell, a grounding bass note giving fullness to the chord.

A hay wagon pulls onto the road ahead of her, and the pace slows to a crawl. The car behind her is trying to pass. Feeling anxious and hemmed in by them both, she pulls the truck into the first driveway she sees, turns around, and heads for home.

CHAPTER 10

The house looks quiet; they may not be home. Even so, she doesn't want to go in. She heads towards the barn and climbs the loft ladder. The worn billfold's still there. Sitting on a hay bale near the open loft door, she takes out the picture. It hasn't changed. The same fierce, clear eyes, the serious mouth and upheld chin stare back at her. But this time she sees it differently. She sees a woman looking beyond the surface of things, beyond the everyday world into another, one that Norma Jean only glimpses at odd moments.

Yes, she thinks, we *are* different. Yet she feels no sense of loss, no disconnection. In the span of one afternoon, her mother has become a person, more real than a longed-for parent, more solid than a fanciful and contrary girl. Julia Taylor was special. But out of place. An extraordinary person in an ordinary world, and somehow, it didn't work out. But she touched lives all the same—Ethel's, Uncle Frank's, Essie's—and she brought her daughter into the world. Best of all, she'd *wanted* to have her, she had held her dear.

Norma Jean sits by the open loft door and looks over the fields, theirs and others beyond, a whole world of fields out there. In her mind she can smell the turned earth and hear the buzzing of bees and June bugs. Her mother must have sat here many times, seen things that are closed to her own eyes. The tree line running along the river reminds her of the hidden sandbar surrounded by honeysuckle and wild roses. And it reminds her of the drowning. Accident or suicide? She's not even been able to ask the question before; it was too awful to consider. Somehow, right now, the answer doesn't matter. An exceptional young woman gave life to her; now it's up to her to live it. Norma Jean smiles, a small smile that grows larger and larger. She thinks of her quilt and knows Julia would love it, the strangeness and craziness of it, the love pocket. It was the Julia in herself that created it.

But how is she different? That's the tinge of excitement she's feeling. *In what ways am I different? What will my life be? Life* is the word. Life is what she's reaching for, to follow her heart—freely. She stands in the loft door and takes a deep breath, feeling such fullness, such buoyancy. Only the earthy smell of the straw, the rough boards beneath her feet keep her from leaping forward, sailing up through the air, far out over the endless fields.

CHAPTER 11

Norma Jean has not given much thought to when or how she will show the completed quilt. In a way she shrinks from exposing her work to the comments of others, her innermost self laid open to public view. But she's also eager to share, excited by the energy the quilt gives her, the strong sense of family. She knows that spreading it out, talking about it is a necessary part of this process.

116

The aroma of roses fills the yard and the house. A large vase of pink, peach, and yellow blooms sits on a table near Gram, and Norma Jean has cut her own bouquet and carried them up to the attic in a Mason jar. She sits on an old trunk looking at the quilt, breathing in the rose perfume along with her own contentment.

Without giving it much thought, she begins to remove the quilt from the frame, folding it end to end until she has a bundle she can easily carry. She holds it next to her face, feeling the soft material against her cheek, then makes her way down the narrow attic steps, past the bedrooms off the upstairs hall, and down the staircase that leads to the ground floor. Aunt Edna's working in the vegetable garden out back, and Gram is tucked in the old wing chair near the window where she can look out at the rose garden when she's not sleeping.

Norma Jean smooths back Gram's hair, stoops down to take a listless hand in her own and rub it against her cheek. When the old woman's expressionless eyes turn in her direction, she extends her other arm displaying the folded quilt. Gram looks at it blankly at first, but Norma Jean senses she is studying the quilt, confused by its strange familiarity.

She waits a few minutes, before she stands and half unfolds the quilt, revealing the love pocket. An immediate response flickers across Gram's face, and her eyes, so long vacant, focus intently on the love pocket—puzzled, frowning, and finally softening. Placing the quilt on her lap, Norma Jean watches as she passes her fingers over the velvety squares, lightly strokes the border of roses. When she looks up, her eyes are teary but not sad, and her lips move silently to form a word that can only be "Julia."

Any uncertainty Norma Jean had felt about making this quilt, any hesitation about showing it to her family and others is erased by Gram's response. Perhaps Aunt Edna was right to protect her at first. Certainly the trauma of having her world turned upside down so suddenly, of losing her husband and her daughter, one steady as an anchor, the other variable as a breeze, would have a deep effect. It seems to Norma Jean there are those people in the world who are solid and

117

steady, unquestioning in their ways like Aunt Edna and Grandpa, and, in his own way, Uncle Frank. There are those like her mother and Gram whose spirit is lighter, more spontaneous, more vulnerable.

And where is *she*? How does *she* want to be? Alive and spirited as Aggie and Julia? Solid and focused like Travis and Edna? Quiet and steady as Frank?

I have all this in me, all this and maybe something else—a determination to go my own way, accept the risks, and be who I am. Could this be the gift of my father?

***

Aunt Edna, Uncle Frank, and Norma Jean are sitting at the kitchen table for their noon dinner.

"Big headlines in the paper today," says Uncle Frank. "No more separated schools! The court says it ain't constitutional."

"Oh," says Norma Jean. "Does that mean we'll have one school for everybody in the county? I mean, one high school and one elementary school for all the students?"

Aunt Edna shakes her head. "That's just not going to work around here. Folks are too set in their opinions about such things. And where's the money coming from?"

"I don't see how it matters that much," muses Norma Jean. "How's it that different from farm kids going to school with town or city kids? How was it for you, Uncle Frank, when you came in from the country to go to school in town?"

"Well, I didn't know anybody much, of course, and their clothes looked different—cleaner, you know, and newer. I was used to just running around barefoot, wearing my overalls. I remember the boy who sat in front of me—his hair all slicked back every morning, and he wore a different shirt every day of the week."

"But that's not the main thing," Aunt Edna broke in. "Their whole *life* is different, their family life and the way they talk and eat, the way they *learn*—and what they have and haven't learned, too."

118

Norma Jean thinks of the colored children she's seen playing around the AME church on Sundays—how lively and laughing they seem, like rainbows in their bright-colored ribbons and dresses.

"Well," says Uncle Frank, "I know a lot of folks won't like it. I hear the things some of them say about 'different races' and 'each in his own place.' Some folks talk about the Negroes like they're animals that need to be trained but aren't capable of being equal citizens. Some say things a lot meaner than that. But I worked many a day alongside them in the fields, hoeing, picking beans and cotton or such. I think I'd a-been just fine going to the same school. As to trouble coming, I 'spect you're right. 'Can't make an omelet without breaking eggs.'

Norma Jean sits quietly, applying that saying to herself. Graduation's right around the corner, and she's about to break out of the restrictive but protective shell of her family, her quilting group, Pine Grove.

***

The quilting circle meets later as the days lengthen, gathering at seven and leaving in twilight at nine. The cooing sounds of the doves, who have taken up summer residence in the church bell tower, float down through the open windows, and the fragrances of summer—roses, honeysuckle, mint—come and go with the breeze.

Norma Jean walks into the room, the last to arrive, holding her quilt with only the backing visible. She is smiling and Ethel Posey and Miss Ella Mae smile also, looking up at her expectantly. Bea's lips are pursed, her expression skeptical.

The table they work around is still clear, and Norma Jean unfolds the quilt spreading it out before them. Almost at once all three women stand up to get a better view. They look at the quilt as Norma Jean looks at their faces, and for a while no one says a word. Then shaking her head and smiling a broad smile, Miss Ella Mae looks up. "Child, what have you got here? You have done something so new and different I can't take it all in. But I know it's wonderful, just wonderful."

119

"It's new and old at the same time," says Ethel, a broad smile on her face. "Like taking the seeds from a garden long established and planting them somewhere different—and in an entirely different way. How did you ever come up with it?"

Bea is staring, her mouth hanging open. "Well, there sure has never been anything like this in Pine Grove—or anywhere else for all I know. What planet did you get it from, Norma Jean? And what's it about? I can't make any sense of it."

Norma Jean looks down at her quilt. There's such a hodgepodge of fabrics from times past, such an absence of symmetry in the design. But there is movement—undeniable movement and flow across the surface, lower left to upper right, and she feels the flow in her body, running through her blood, expanding her breath. On the quilt face she sees and knows her own life, separate yet connected to her family history, to the history of all families everywhere.

"What will you do with such a thing?" asks Bea. "Hang it on your bedroom wall? It would scare me to death, give me all kinds of dreams."

Though she hasn't considered this question, Norma Jean speaks without hesitation. "This quilt will be part of my everyday living. It'll lie on my bed," she says running her hand across its surface, "where I can see it and touch it, lie down on top of it to write or read. And in winter," she laughs, "it will cover me up, keep me snug and warm."

"It's a fine piece of work, Norma Jean," says Miss Ella Mae as she leans over to examine the stitches. "Whatever you do with it, it will last a long time, throughout your life and some generations to come. I'm proud to be quilting with you, to witness your growing and your work."

Ethel, nodding in agreement, looks up at Norma Jean. "You know, this is what we do when we're quilting, use scraps and pieces of our lives and bring them together in some kind of order, some sort of completeness. Maybe that's what makes quilting so satisfying. And this one is your own expression, Norma Jean, your creation, yours alone. Yes, indeed, it's a very fine piece of work."

120

Norma Jean feels her eyes misting up as she looks at the women around the circle, a group that has meant so much to her. "Well," she says, "I couldn't have done any of it without all of you. Wherever I go, this circle will always be in my heart. I'll think of you sitting here every Tuesday night.

"And," she smiles, "I'll even think of someone else sitting in my chair, sharing and sewing—someone like Minnie Lewis who'd fit right in."

Bea's eyes grow wide with alarm, but Miss Ella May and Ethel are happy and smiling.

***

Graduation day is hot and humid. Families sit on folding chairs in the school gym facing the temporary stage, wiping their brows and trying to stir a breeze with cardboard fans from Maley's Funeral Parlor. The graduates are lined up in the corridor, sweltering in their long robes and feeling a mixture of eagerness and bewilderment as they proceed from the familiar structure of school into a hazy future.

As they file into the gym, "Pomp and Circumstance" ringing in their ears, Norma Jean thinks of Shirleen, how she would love all this ceremony, be smiling and waving to the audience, probably giggling with her partner as they marched up the double aisle. She *is* graduating, but right now she's supposed to be visiting her relatives in Ohio, "helping to care for her sick aunt," Mrs. Miller reported. She'll get her diploma by mail and attend a small junior college in the fall. She and Norma Jean have a regular correspondence going, and Norma Jean's been pleased with the upbeat tone of her friend's letters, the old Shirleen bouncing with enthusiasm and possibilities. But no echo of worries or regrets. She suspects this will be the tone of all their exchanges; Shirleen's not one to look deeper.

Norma Jean's feelings are mixed, today, a blend of relief and anticipation. She's definitely ready to move on now, and her quilt, and everything it means to her, will move with her. But when she looks out from the stage and sees Aunt Edna and Uncle Frank, a lump rises in her

121

throat. Uncle Frank looks hot and uncomfortable in his Sunday church suit, but he's grinning from ear to ear. "You know," he said proudly at breakfast, "this is my first graduation."

Aunt Edna is sitting upright, as she usually does, her mouth pursed but her head nodding in approval, her strength of character visible and unshakeable. *They will always be here for me*, Norma Jean thinks, *like bedrock, a bedrock foundation.*

***

The sky is pure blue with a few puffs of white clouds. "A lazy summer day," Neill says as they drive down the road, "perfect for the river."

Norma Jean feels a little weird riding along in Neill's truck with nothing on but a bathing suit and a loose shirt. She looks back at the canoe resting in the truck bed, rocking a bit with the bumps. Maybe the ride on the water will be smoother, she thinks. Maybe. But on the road there's solid ground beneath. You can count on that, even if it's bumpy.

She thinks of the day she finally met Neill's parents—a planned "drop-in" after a movie. His mother, overly polite but never once looking her in the eye or asking about her plans for after graduation. And Dr. Thompson, stiff and serious, his fingers tapping some unheard rhythm on the arm of his chair.

Neill looks her way and smiles. "Don't worry," he says, "this canoe's an old friend. We'll glide across the water smooth as silk."

Now it's her turn to smile. She has known him for six months, and it still amazes her how easily he seems to flow with everything, how this makes it all seem easier for her.

He turns down a dusty farm road that runs between a cornfield and the river. They can see the water now, sunlight playing over its surface and reflecting along the far bank. On their side, the bank is clear of brush. It all looks so different from the Black River that Norma Jean knows; she wonders for a moment if Neill, aware of her mother's drowning, has decided to bring her to a different place.

122

"Hold on," he says as they hit a couple of deep ruts. "There're some good launching places along here. We'll be on the water soon."

They are upriver from the Taylor farm, five miles or so. The plan is to paddle down to the bridge, tie up the canoe, and walk or catch a ride the three miles back to the farm. They'll use Uncle Frank's truck to return to the launching place where Neill will get his truck, retrieve the boat, and follow Norma Jean home.

"How wide will the river get?"

"Oh, you'll be more surprised by how narrow it gets. Some places you can nearly touch bushes on both banks."

CHAPTER 12

The river is full but slow-moving, almost languid where they put in. Neill helps her into the front of the canoe; she holds on tight to the rim as the boat wobbles when he steps in the back.

"Can't I sit in the back?" Norma Jean asks. Up front feels unprotected; anything could lie ahead.

"I have to sit back here to steer. You look out for branches and tree trunks sticking out from the banks or just under the water. And paddle, of course. We both have to paddle."

They start downstream. Norma Jean notices how lightly they move over the water, weightless as a leaf. It's quiet, too. The only sounds are their paddles lifting the water and occasional birdcalls from along the bank. They glide through a new world, dappled and liquid, incredibly calm and still. The flickering sunlight and a few floating sticks and grasses are all they see moving, and she breathes it in deeply, relaxing into the surroundings.

Ahead the stream narrows, just as Neill predicted. Soon foliage surrounds them, and Norma Jean is suddenly busy pushing the canoe away from exposed, twisted roots and ducking the overhanging limbs.

"You okay?" asks Neill, righting himself after lying back flat on the boat to skim under a low branch.

"Oh, yeah," she laughs, pushing them away from a sandbar with her paddle, then reaching quickly to the other side to avoid a snag. "And a few minutes ago I was thinking how tranquil the river is."

"Did you see that high water mark along the trees? When it's up there, you have a different river, one you'd never call tranquil."

A different river.

**

They've been paddling about an hour, when the river widens and a sandbar appears on the right, a good place, says Neill, to pull up and eat lunch. The canoe thuds onto the sand, and Norma Jean jumps out to steady the bow, glad to feel the ground beneath her and to stretch her stiff legs.

"Where are we, Neill? Whose farm are we near?" Only riverbank and sky are visible. She's lost her bearings.

"We're on the river, Norma Jean. That's all you can really say. No sign posts out here. We're on a soft, shady bank on a beautiful summer's day. What else do we need to know?"

She looks over at him, his easy stance, his kind, amused eyes, his tan body shiny with sweat and oil. 'A soft, shady bank on a beautiful summer's day.' She imagines her young mother and father on another sandbar eighteen years earlier. A mixture of all the feelings she's ever known—sadness and joy, laughter, tears, yearning. tenderness, confusion—converge and swell inside her, turbulent as rapids after a hard rain. Is it love? She feels lightheaded, her legs wobbly as sand.

"You all right?" Neill says, reaching out to steady her. He runs a finger over a rough scratch on her arm. "You were good keeping us out of those branches."

Norma Jean takes hold of his hand. "Yes. Yes, I'm all right. It's just . . . it's not what I expected." She looks off down the river. "I was scared at first, of the river, of what happened here. But . . . it's a long

124

river, isn't it?" She laughs. "This last part has been so busy . . . it's, well, it's fun. I wouldn't want to do it alone, but . . . my mother, what happened to my mother, that was so long ago. Now that we're out here, it doesn't seem to have much to do with her drowning." She looks up at Neill's face. "You know, I think of her often as *Julia*. That's what everyone calls her; it seems to fit her free-spirit. If she *had* run off with my father—or even if she hadn't—and if Gram had stayed well, I think Gram would've seemed more like my mother. And that would be okay. That would really be fine."

Neill looks at her half-smiling. The smile fades into something different, more serious. He holds her face and kisses her, softly at first, then with more intention. She feels the tip of his tongue run across her lips; he pulls her close as her arms circle his body. His skin feels warm and smooth, and her own is alive with sensation. This is new territory, a voice warns from far inside her, while the whole rest of her wants to stay there forever.

"Geez," says Neill, pulling slightly away. "Norma Jean, I never . . . well, I never felt so . . . ." His face is flushed, and he swallows hard like he can't get out the words. Suddenly, he grabs her hand. "Come on," he says, "let's jump in the water."

"What?"

"It's not deep here. We've never been swimming together. Come on, the river's waiting for us."

"O.K.," she says, "O.K.," and runs splashing in beside him. Her feet sink into the soft muddy bottom, the sun hits her face, and her body, invigorated by the cool water, feels one hundred percent alive. The dark river flows slowly by, sparkles of sunlight dancing across the surface.

CHAPTER 13

2013

A light breeze rustles the leaves, just beginning to show a bit of orange and gold. A field of drying cornstalks stands off to the left, and beyond them, a long line of geese head south over the river. It all feels familiar, so familiar, and at the same time unreal, as though she were floating between two worlds—the Taylor farm of her growing up years, and this *Country Inn B & B* where, after some sixty years, she's now a "paying guest." In one sense it seems she should be shelling peas with an old newspaper spread out in her lap. In another she feels like an undercover intruder, who knows the bones of this place better than any of the other people here could imagine.

She reads a write-up someone has sent her from the *Jackson Herald* and can't quit thinking about it, even to the point of having nagging discussions with herself.

"Why *not* go back? Aren't you curious?"

"Well, yes, in a way; but I remember it like it *was*. Won't it be sad and upsetting to see it all changed?"

"But that was years ago! Everything changes—either moves forward or dies. You've always believed that."

"I know, I know. But this was my base, my touchstone. Maybe my mind's eye is reluctant to let go of that."

"Or to see it anew and different?"

That grounded, practical "voice" sounds familiar—Neill? Ethel Posey? They were certainly touchstones in her life—even her life beyond Pine Grove. Norma Jean has not had what one would call an *eventful* life, a particularly *exciting* one. But *fulfilling*—Yes! She has gotten to do exactly what she most wanted—to work with babies, unwanted babies, and with the new parents who adopted them. She has made more baby quilts than she can count, her aim, to send each baby to their new home with their own little quilt.

There aren't many people she knows in Pine Grove any more, and the town itself is different. Jackson has prospered and spread, become one of several that have attracted folks who work in the city, but don't want to live there. Developers, quick to recognize an opportunity, bought up farms as they became available and built subdivisions, golf courses, even small shopping centers. The buildings

126

on Main Street are relatively the same, but the stores are different, more up-to-date shops, a beauty salon, a couple of trendy restaurants, home decor boutiques—even a massage salon. Black faces mingle with white ones along the street now, and when she passes the old confederate statue as she heads for the cemetery, she wonders how long it will continue to stand in honor of a slave-holding South.

School integration was just starting when she left Pine Grove, and the tension that surrounded it had affected everyone. Her own small quilting group had dissolved shortly after she left, when Miss Ella Mae brought Minnie Lewis to the church one Wednesday evening. Bea Jones had gathered up her scrap bag and marched out in a huff. Then the church members themselves had long painful discussions about whether God intended for their own congregation to be mixed or separate. She wishes both Ethel Posey and Miss Ella Mae had lived to see the opening of the Pine Grove Clinic that serves *everyone* in their community—regardless of the color of their skin. And she wishes Essie had lived to hear the cry of "Black Lives Matter."

The cemetery still holds its old peaceful atmosphere. She lets herself sink into it as she walks the shaded paths; over sixty years, and it hardly seems changed at all—the head stone for Gram next to Grandpa Travis, and the simple stones for Aunt Edna and Uncle Frank, her mother, Julia. All these lives, once so real and busy, now at rest in this place of trees, wildflowers, bird songs. She walks past the stone bench where she had tried to comfort Shirleen but only upset her. Shirleen had been right about one thing that day. Norma Jean had no idea how it felt to be pregnant and scared, to feel your own body changing, harboring an intruder, and not knowing which way to turn or what to do about it.

We were all so ignorant then, she thinks, *so aware of people's expectations and so unaware of our place in it*. Even herself, setting out to comfort unwed mothers who were hidden off from society, cast out like lepers, burdened with shame. Her own vocation has changed drastically over the years—the freedom of the sixties, the women's movement. Being pregnant is no longer something you try to cover up. Maternity clothes have become whatever's comfortable; "showing" is a

127

non-issue. Having a baby is merely part of being a woman; being adopted, no longer a big secret.

Her own career has bridged this change. Young unmarried mothers now openly *decide* whether or not to keep their babies. And if they do, there is no stigma against working outside the home and pursuing one's own career at the same time.

Shirleen, of course, had given up her baby, not even considered keeping it. Norma Jean smiles trying to imagine Shirleen pushing a baby carriage, warming a bottle on the stove. She'd met a "fabulous guy" in Ohio where she had stayed with her aunt. Her letter to Norma Jean was full of superlatives—*good-looking, fun, ambitious and sooo well-off.* They had married and settled down in an "amazing" house in a wealthy Cleveland suburb. There were occasional postcards from romantic places—Lake Tahoe, Bermuda, New York City. No children. But she had channeled her old enthusiasm into Junior League projects, charity fashion shows, boating on Lake Erie—a life light years away from Pine Grove.

Not so with Neill. There were long confiding letters from his college as she completed her own training. Searching questions about difficult decisions at each crossroads, fears and hopes. They used each other as sounding boards, even after they had each married and settled into family life. He *did* become a lawyer, eventually a legislator, and always an advocate for the rights of the suppressed. *Yes*, thought Norma Jean, *he has been the continuous touchstone in my life*.

And what a full rich life it has been! Finding the right home for infant orphans has been her heart's delight. And through experience and training, through observation and asking the right questions, she has become very good at it, would happily devote her whole life to it. But then comes Devin.

To Norma Jean all babies are beautiful, sweet, immediately lovable, but she has to admit that Devin does not fall in those categories. Scrawny, wrinkled, red-faced, with wisps of dark hair shooting off in every direction, and a sharp-edged cry that won't stop. His mother, Lona, a sickly and undernourished-looking young woman, shows up on the doorstep of their facility just days before her delivery, depressed and scared and unwilling to communicate. Despite numerous attempts to trace her background no one comes forward to offer information. After the birth, she never regains consciousness, never sees her baby.

They feed him and tend him, give him as much attention as they can, but his growth is slow, much slower than most babies, and his looks so unappealing, Norma Jean wonders if anyone will ever adopt him. Hoping that more consistent personal contact might reassure him, she gets permission to keep him in a small crib near her desk where he can see her face and hear her voice often throughout the day. He seems to improve—taking more milk from his bottle, sleeping less fitfully. But just as they are considering his readiness for adoption, the doctor, who comes weekly to check the infants, notices his legs—not developing in the usual way, oddly turned and out of proportion with the rest of his body. The diagnosis is unclear.

It all comes together for Norma Jean. Here is a child no one wants, who will end up in an institution. She can't let that happen. The very thought of it makes her panic. Without realizing it, she has become irrevocably attached to Devin. He looks at her with his deep blue eyes, and she knows they belong together.

It isn't easy for a single woman to adopt a child at this time— many applications to fill out, numerous interviews, trial periods, and inspections. She is working at an adoption agency in Roanoke and makes several trips to the state capital in Richmond to plead her case. On one of them she finds herself in the waiting room of the office of Robert Cravens, deputy assistant to the person in charge of the state-wide program. When the secretary opens the door, she is surprised to see the man behind the desk sitting in a wheel chair. He is a good listener, unhurried, attentive. He has her career history, promotions, letters of recommendation in front of him, but his questions seem more personal, as if he is weighing emotional attachment to the child as well as her judgment.

"You know, Miss Taylor, that Devin's future is unclear. He may or may not improve. He could spend the rest of his life, well," he says, with a simple gesture towards his own legs, "in a wheel chair, and he's only a young boy. Have you a realistic notion of what kind of care this could involve?"

Norma Jean smiles broadly as she thinks of Gram, and words tumble out of her as she relives those years of caring for her grandmother on the farm, of learning to quilt at her feet, of coaxing her to eat, wrapping her in warm quilts in winter beside the big fireplace, and opening windows in summer to allow the scent of peaches and roses to drift in.

She stops abruptly, a bit embarrassed when she sees the look on his face, a combination of attentiveness and amazement.

"Miss Taylor," he says, "Miss Norma Jean Taylor. I'm sure in your work of matching parents with children, always with every hope of success, once in a while you've found a match that seemed, well, made in heaven in its rightness. Of *course*, you must have Devin; of course, you two belong together. I'll do everything I can to see that it happens."

And with that he wheels his chair around the desk and reaches out to shake her hand.

Afterwards, there are letters, phone calls, visits—and not all of them official. Within the year, she and Robert Cravens are married. They become a family.

Norma Jean feels her eyes mist up, more with gratefulness than sadness. She has outlived almost everyone, but they still live deep inside of her. All the aspects of her family seem to merge and coalesce—Robert and Devin, Grandpa Travis, her mother Julia, her unknown father, and Gram, Aunt Edna and Uncle Frank—even the extended family she imagined from their clothing in the attic. All seem a part of one piece, like the family quilt she made by piecing together those she loved into one warm and familiar cover.

MRS. FERRY

I first began watching Mrs. Ferry because she scared me, scared me half to death. She was the biggest woman I'd ever seen, not just tall or fat, but *big*. And the white uniform made her look bigger. I stood there in the lunch line in front of her on the first day of school with my mouth hanging open. "Keep moving, keep moving," the lunch-ticket-lady called from the end of the line, and Mrs. Ferry reached right over the big steam table—the edge made a deep crease in her white-aproned stomach—and dumped a whole spoonful of peas and carrots on top of my mashed potatoes. I don't like mashed potatoes much, and I *hate* green peas, can't stand the sight of them. But I didn't say a word. "Move on," someone said, and I did, though my knees were shaking.

The smell of those big canned peas made me feel sick. Our teacher, Miss Helen, wouldn't let us waste food. "You eat what you take," she said. It was war time, WWII, and there was lots of talk about "waste not" and "starving children in Europe." So after eating the fish sticks, I tried to hide the peas in the mashed potatoes and pecked at the carrots. They tasted like peas. In third grade we studied food families, and Miss Helen had told us to use these names in the cafeteria for practice. So I pushed it all under a slice of bread and said I was too full to eat any more starch. As I scraped it all into the metal garbage can, I saw Mrs. Ferry looking at me, her fat arms across her chest. My face turned hot.

And school was just starting! I had to walk through the lunch line everyday and go past Mrs. Ferry. I didn't want to see her. I especially didn't want her to look at me. I was small and skinny for my age, almost lost in dresses that always felt too big. My face stayed half hidden behind the bangs of my long, straight hair. I was shy. My only security was my purse, a clutch bag of soft blue velvet that held my lunch ticket, a nickel or two, a flowered handkerchief, and the rabbit's foot I'd won at the county fair. I could touch it whenever I reached inside. My purse was always with me.

I tried to slip through the lunch line unnoticed, tried to imagine myself invisible. But no matter where I stood in line or how I walked or ducked my head, my eyes always came in contact with Mrs. Ferry's. She was like a magnet, a huge white moon, so fixed and enormous that I was compelled to look at her even though I cringed away.

Mrs. Ferry never spoke, but whatever she served I was bound to receive. Her big ham-like hand reached out for my plate. I hesitated a moment, then passed it up to her. I can still feel her sure grip on the opposite side of that heavy, white plate as she plopped down a big spoonful of succotash or a salmon croquet. Then she looked right at me, hard. That look spoke to me. It said: "Eat!"

Mrs. Ferry was never absent. She piled my plate with huge portions and strange mixtures. I looked at the menu board each day with dread. I could always tell what Mrs. Ferry would be serving: applesauce, beets, creamed tuna—whatever I hated most. There wasn't much food I liked anyway, but there were things I detested. Mushy things. Mushy things combined with crisp or crumbly things. Anything seeping fat.

There was no escaping Mrs. Ferry. Perhaps with my skinny wrists and furtive glances, I reminded her of war orphans, undernourished and insecure. Other students could pass her unnoticed, but when I came by, she heaped it on.

Between her helpings and Miss Helen's clean-plate policy, I was trapped. The bread trick was soon discovered. Once I wrapped some awful Brussels sprouts in my handkerchief and slipped them in my blue purse to dump out later. I had to sprinkle it with bath powder to get rid of the smell. My plate was loaded each day, and each day I ate. I ate tiny bites so I could swallow quickly without tasting. I tried large bites to get it all down sooner. I hid despised morsels in larger, less despised ones so they wouldn't touch my tongue, peas hidden in potatoes, apple sauce camouflaged between slices of bread.

The cafeteria was in the basement, small for a school dining room, with low ceilings and a few high basement windows. The light above the dining area was dim for wartime conservation, but the light in the kitchen, which was sectioned off by the serving tables, was brighter. Our class sat right in front of this area, and throughout the lunch period,

134

I could see Mrs. Ferry. Her broad, tank-like face and her white-uniformed bosom mushroomed above the counter of the steamy kitchen.

I began to have a weird dream, the same dream again and again. I was at the corner of a big sheet, a huge white canopy that billowed upward and outward through an endless nighttime sky. I looked up across its white surface, awed and fascinated, but feeling very small. It waved and rippled, beckoning me forward, and I leaned toward it feeling its pull sweep through me like a gale. Then a silent buzzing started way back in my head, a dizzying fear of being drawn into the whiteness. With a gasp I sat up in bed.

* * *

In the cafeteria, I was eating. To counter the effects of Mrs. Ferry's food, I was putting more items on my plate. Fruit salad took the edge off sickening sauces. Anything lost its identity in macaroni and cheese. Cornbread concealed even the taste and feel of okra. I glanced up to see if she noticed, but her expression was unchanged. All this food had its effect. My face was filling out. The mirror image that looked back at me between those straight strands of dark hair seemed bolder, less inclined to hide. My wrists were still toothpicks that classmates could handcuff with a thumb and forefinger, but my arms were stronger. Often I could pull away.

In an effort to avoid Mrs. Ferry's gaze, as well as the sight of my plate, I began to pay more attention to the kids around me at the lunch table. Billy Watts, a large loud boy who talked with his mouth full and slurped his milk, intimidated me. He was full of wisecracks and would call out to me across the table, things like "Hey, Shrimp, quit hogging the salt." But one day he imitated the principal, bugging out his eyes, sucking in his cheeks, rolling his head to one side. I began to giggle behind my hand, and when he added a nasal "Good morning students," I laughed out loud.

And Kathy Morrow who sat beside me, who seemed so sure of herself, so perfect with long blonde hair like a princess, began to tell me secrets. She whispered about her family, how her father had left home, how her mother was always crying, how she didn't know what to do,

135

just stayed in her room reading and drawing. She wrote me long notes that began to fill up my purse.

Even Mrs. Ferry began to get some of my willing attention. Screened off a bit by classmates, I glanced up at her from my place at the table, more from interest now than fear. From that viewpoint I couldn't see her arms, only her wide face with flat, pulled-back hair like a dark halo. She stood behind the stream of bobbing heads that inched by, her expression never changing, her mouth never smiling, her eyes never narrowing or widening, never showing anything. She could have been frozen. I still recoiled when I was opposite her in line, like the time at the ocean when a giant wave hung just above my head for a moment before crashing down. I was still helpless before the strong arm that reached toward my tray, the long metal spoon that dropped its food with a clang on my plate, sending a tiny vibration through my hand, connecting me like invisible fishing line with the leviathan.

But at the table, distanced a bit, she was less fearsome. Once Billy referred to her as "old ferry boat," and I laughed at the way that fit her size and her steady, unhurried servings. But when another boy called her "ferret-face," I was annoyed. That was mean and didn't fit at all. I quickly looked up, hoping she hadn't heard.

I had thought she didn't look at the other students so hard the way she looked at me, thought she simply stared over the tops of their heads. Or did she? Was it just that the other students were jostling and talking, not looking back at her? Maybe she gave them the same look that I myself encountered, the only difference being that I encountered it.

I began to notice things about Mrs. Ferry. She seldom talked to the other cafeteria ladies. Just a nod or word about the food, but never chatter or a laugh. Mrs. Price who ran the lunch room hustled around the kitchen directing the workers, checking the food, moving us along. Mrs. Cobb, stern and set on keeping order, was forever lecturing us on how we should behave.

Mrs. Ferry was not a part of this. She neither fussed nor joked. I wondered if she was always this way. I had never seen her outside the dining room, never seen her in a coat or on the street, had no idea of the house she lived in or the family she had. I could no more imagine her somewhere else than I could imagine the big lunchroom refrigerator in a seat at the movie theater or in line at the grocery store.

This thought struck me so hard that I imagined something else. I imagined that the real-life Mrs. Ferry was a different person altogether, smaller, brown-haired, a shy and gentle woman who hid inside the stone-like body of Mrs. Ferry-of-the-lunchroom. Arriving early before the other workers, she opened up the Ferry-suit, stepped inside the huge mannequin, and snapped it shut. Then she stationed herself at the serving table and dispensed her food. Each night, the last to leave, she stepped out and left her costume parked behind the counter till the next morning. During the day she never spoke because she was timid and afraid of being found out, of losing her job. She spoke silently only to me because I was small and uneasy like herself.

Of course I knew this was just a made-up idea, and I could probably get some admiring giggles if I told it at the table. But I didn't want to tell. It was our secret, mine and Mrs. Ferry's. I wouldn't give it away.

***

One day when we went into the lunch room, there was a message in the center of the menu board. Beneath the yellow-chalked offerings of the day—creamed chipped beef, lima beans, bread pudding—were big words in blue chalk: THANKS AND GOODBYE TO MRS. FERRY. I was stunned. Mrs. Ferry stood at her usual place behind the counter wielding her spoon and wearing her usual blank expression. The words on the board seemed as unrelated to her as she did to her surroundings, and I looked again to make sure I had really seen the message.

"Hey, Ferry's leaving," Billy called out. "They must need a white elephant at the zoo."

"Maybe she's joining the circus," another boy said. "Live and in Person, the Abominable Snowwoman!"

137

"Shh!" warned Kathy. "She'll hear you!"

We were getting close to her serving place, and the boys quieted down to giggles. I wanted to ask where she was going and why, but I couldn't speak. Mrs. Ferry filled her spoon and held out her hand for my plate. The boys nudged me, and I moved on in the line.

There was a lot of joking and talking at the table that day, and I pretty much dropped Mrs. Ferry from my mind.

"Hey, Goldilocks," Billy yelled over to Kathy, "where'd you leave the three bears? Stuffed in Shrimpy's pouch?" He winked at me, and I felt a blush covering my face. Kathy nudged me with her elbow. "See," she said, "he likes you." But then he grabbed the blue purse from my lap and tossed it like a basketball to a boy across the table.

When Miss Helen warned us to quiet down, I looked up and tried to imagine Mrs. Ferry *not* being there. I couldn't. It was like imagining my house not being in the middle of our block.

Soon the lunch bell rang, and we streamed up the steps leaving thoughts of the dimmed cafeteria behind. But when school was over and I was gathering my belongings, I couldn't find my purse.

"Maybe you left it in the lunchroom," said Billy grinning in a mischievous way.

"Don't worry," said Miss Helen, "anything they find will be put out on the table by the menu board. You can get it on the way out."

The cafeteria steps were at the end of the hall just inside the back door of the school. A short flight of steps went down to the landing, then turned and descended to the lunchroom. I ran down the first flight, hurrying so I could catch up with my friends, but at the landing my pace got slower. The cafeteria lights were off. It looked shadowy down there, and my footsteps sounded hollow in the empty stairwell. When I reached the bottom step, I saw it was not completely dark. The small oblong windows near the ceiling let in some light, and a florescent bar glowed in the kitchen above the stove. I could hear the refrigerator humming.

138

Trailing my hand along the tile wall, I made my way towards the menu board. My heart was thumping, and I thought how odd it was that my friends, who must be laughing and teasing just above these windows, seemed miles away.

"You lookin' fur this?"

I froze like a startled rabbit. The flat voice had come from the dim seating area, and as I looked, I could see a figure seated at the end of our table. She was wearing a dark buttoned coat and knitted hat, but I knew, before my eyes could make out her face, that it was Mrs. Ferry. She was hunched over, her weight resting on her arms and her hands folded together. In front of them was my blue purse.

"Y-y-yes," I said. "Yes ma'am. I left it here. At lunch time."

I stood where I was, didn't even think of moving. She looked at me like she was looking through me, through the wall, and through the whole rest of my life. A few moments passed that seemed like a long time. Mrs. Ferry slowly scraped back her chair. Then she pressed her large hands on the edge of the table and pushed herself up.

"Better take it then," she said.

She picked it up along with her own big bag, and I slowly walked forward and held out my hand. She placed the purse in it, and my fingers closed around the soft, familiar fabric. For a few moments we both held on, her hand covering the top, my palm hidden by the pouch.

"Thank you," I said in a voice I hardly heard. "Thank you. Goodbye, Mrs. Ferry." Our eyes met as she slowly nodded her head.

"Best hold on to what's your'n," she said, releasing the purse. Then stood there, still and silent.

"Yes ma'am," I answered faintly. "I will."

I turned and walked across to the stairwell, then fairly flew up the steps. My heart was beating fast, and I wanted to get outside and see the sky. My friends had thrown down their books and were playing around the jungle gym. I ran over to join them, grabbed the bars, and climbed right up to the top.

139

A few minutes later I glanced toward the road and saw the retreating back of Mrs. Ferry, broad and erect, moving slowly down the sidewalk. I watched her go and grow smaller in the distance. Then I lifted my arms up to the breeze above my head, feeling light and airy as a bird. Only my knees, locked tight around the metal bars, kept me from flying away.

THE LOVE SEAT

They saw it on Friday on the road home from Brownsville, an old-fashioned love seat right out there straddling the center line. It was turned over with its hind legs sticking up in the air "like a donkey," Cletis said, but Earline recognized it before they even came to a stop.

"My lord in heaven," she gasped, "it's Miz Baptist's love seat."

"It's *what?*"

"The love seat—from her front parlor. Don't look at me like I'm crazy, Cletis, I've dusted it every week for five years. I ought to know."

Cletis shook his head. "Well then maybe you know what in tarnation it's doing out here in the middle of Rt. 7 where any fool could run into it and get hisself killed."

He got out of the truck, slamming the door so hard blue paint chips flew off the rusted edges, and started pulling the love seat off the road. Earline slid out her side, almost landing in a drain ditch, and hurried around the truck.

"Wait, Cletis, wait, you'll scratch it to pieces. Hold on a minute. It's old."

"I can tell that." He stopped dragging, but still held on to the legs. "Probably headed for the dump down there. People'll dump anything, anywhere on this road. I bet it fell off a truck, and they couldn't be bothered loading it back on."

"No, no, that's not it. This here's what Miz Baptist calls an *airloom*, something's been in her family a long time. She wants to get new covers on the cushion part. I seen the little bits of cloth she was choosing from."

"Well, I ain't toting this thing all the way back to Brownsville, not for Miz airloom Baptist or nobody. But I am getting it off the road." He gave it another heave.

"Cletis, sugar, it's gonna rain soon, just look at the sky. And that ditch's so close to the road, the wind could blow it right in. Just load it up, honey. We can put it on the porch till somebody comes for it." She ducked her chin and gave him her puppy dog look, the one that'd got to him when they first met, but he'd since come to be wary of.

"Please."

"Shit," he said, picking up the two legs on his side while she hefted the other. She was a strong woman with some breadth to her— "pleasantly plump," she liked to say—almost eclipsing his wiry frame. "Next thing you'll be wanting me to pick up cow pies and haul *them* home."

They rattled on down the road, Cletis scowling at the highway ahead, Earline pleased as punch but not daring to say so. She sneaked looks at the love seat through the rear window and felt her heart swell a little, proud to have such a fine piece in the bed of the pickup. When they got to the dirt lane leading up to their tenant house that sat right smack in the middle of Mr. Tipton's cotton field, she got anxious. The ruts in this road could bounce your head to the ceiling if you drove too fast, and she could tell by the look on Cletis' face and the way he shifted the gears, he was going to do just that.

"Stop a minute, honey, hold on." She opened the door and heaved herself out before he could argue. "Cletis," she called from the rear of the truck, "come back here a minute, sweetheart. I need you to help me."

"What in God's name you up to now?" But she already had the tailgate down.

"Just give me a hand here, sugar. I want to steady this settee over the bumps."

Shaking his head, he clasped his hands together and bowed down to give her a foothold. Once on board, she tipped the love seat aright and, spreading her skirts, seated herself in the middle of the faded gold cushion. The cotton fields spread out before her like a kingdom of tiny clouds. Cletis grumped back to the cab, but he drove slow, a coach's pace she imagined, down the length of the dusty lane.

***

144

The love seat looked grand on the front porch; in fact, it perked up the whole house. It was the first thing you saw when you drove towards their place, just sitting there in a way that said *Quality*—at least to Earline. The kids' mouths had gaped open when they saw it.

"Mama," said Jolene who was ten, "it's beautiful." She reached out her hand and hesitantly ran her fingers along the curved glossy wood on top of the back frame.

"Well, what *is* it?" Little Cletis asked. "It's strange looking, ain't it?"

Earline scooped up Baby Joe as he toddled over to look, holding a gummy peppermint stick in his fist. "Ain't that pretty, Baby? You can look and look at it, but no touching, you hear. All you kids. This here's for looking only."

"But, Mama, I want to set on it. Can't I try it, I'm the oldest. I'll be careful."

Earline shook her head, pursing her lips like she meant it. "No indeedy. Y'all hear me? I'll beat your butts so bad you won't sit *any*where for a week. Understand?"

Jolene reluctantly nodded her head.

"Little Cletis?"

"I hear. Who wants to sit on it anyways. Looks hard as a rock."

"We got to keep Baby away. You see him heading for it, just slap his hand. Maybe on Sunday, before we head out for church, I'll let you sit on it for a little bit."

***

Earline called her sister Bernice to come over and perm her hair at the end of the week. "Bring that little camera of yours," said Earline. "I got something to show you. Once you get me all permed, I want you to take a picture."

"Earline," said Cletis, finishing up his mug of coffee in the doorway, "you called Miz Baptist yet? How much longer that thing gonna sit there?"

"Don't you fret, Cletis. They're gone on vacation, won't be back for a couple of weeks. I'm just keeping it safe for them."

***

Two days later they were out in the field picking cotton when a black cloud moved across the sky from the west. It came slow-like, but getting bigger and darker as it went along. When Earline got to the end of her row, she cast a worried look up at the sky.

"Cletis," she called out. She could see him three rows away, but he didn't hear her. She lifted her skirts and huffed over to where he was.

"We got to stop, Cletis. A big one's coming."

Cletis looked up at the cloud as the wind picked up. "Not yet," he said, "too soon. We can get in a couple more rows. Get back to it, now."

"No, no, we can't, Cletis. That rain'll blow every which way. You know how it does when it looks like this."

"You afeared of getting wet all of a sudden?" he asked without raising his head.

"Lord no, not me. I'll dry out, but the love seat—we got to move it in. It'll be ruined if it gets soaked."

Now Cletis raised his head and gave her an unbelieving look. "What? What's that you saying? I'm out here trying to get a crop in, and you're worrying about some old junk furniture? Where's your senses, woman? It won't fit through that door anyways. Just keep picking. We'll throw something over it."

"Cletis, we ain't got nothing to throw over it, nothing that'll keep it dry. Please, baby, you got to help me. We can turn it catty-cornered and get it through. But I can't do it by myself without banging it up."

"For Gawd's sake," said Cletis, grabbing up his bag. "I wish I'd smashed right through that thing when it was on the road. Air-loom, my ass. Get moving."

***

146

It was a struggle, but they made it, twisting and turning it ever which way, Cletis cussing and Earline calling, "Watch out" and "Be careful," the kids standing by wide-mouthed, Jolene holding Baby and biting her lip almost to pieces. Finally, Cletis had to take the front door off its hinges. The last bit of the love seat went through just as the rain blew up. Earline and the kids cheered while Cletis got soaked putting the door back on.

"Where do you want the danged thing?" he asked.

They all stood there looking at it, Earline thinking how small it'd looked in Miz Baptist's parlor. Here it was the biggest thing in the room. The cabin itself was small—a kitchen, two bedrooms, and what they called the front room. In it were two armless pieces of an old sectional sofa Bernice had passed on to them, a creaky rocking chair, and a TV, which the kids mostly watched from an old quilt that lay crumpled on the floor.

"Well," said Earline, "hmm, we could move those sofa pieces over beneath the window here on the front wall; then whoever comes in the door will see the love seat right away."

"You do that, we won't be able to see the TV from the sofa without stretching our necks plum around."

"We could move the TV over to that corner by the love seat...."

"Antennae's hooked up to the wall where it is; I ain't moving it."

"Well then, maybe we could..." She stood there in the doorway, her arms folded and resting on her ample stomach, and considered. "I know—we'll throw a bed sheet over it when we want to watch a program, and you and me'll sit on the love seat together—just us, Cletis, not you children." She waved a warning finger in their direction.

"Chrissake, Earline, it's only for a few days. Alright," he sighed, "let's get done with it. You all push."

***

When Bernice walked in a few days later, her jaw dropped open. "Earline, lord a mercy, where'd you get *that*?"

Earline could hardly contain herself. She wished she'd had Bernice's camera in her hand to take a picture of her expression. "You like it? What'd you think, Sis?"

"What do I think? Honey, it's *gorgeous*. It's like ones you see on TV. It's....but where on earth'd it come from?"

Earline beamed. "See," she looked at Cletis who was standing in the kitchen doorway. "I told you she'd like it."

"But where'd you get it?" Bernice was as big as Earline, but taller and slightly cross-eyed. Somehow this, along with her shrill voice, gave her an air of authority.

"Well, you won't believe this, but we found it."

"What? How could you *find*...."

"Yep, that's what we did," said Earline, nodding her head and shooting a sharp glance at Cletis who was shaking his head and looking disgusted. "We found it on the road. Ain't we lucky?"

"Well, finders, keepers," Pa always said. Anybody careless enough to lose a whole piece of furniture, don't deserve it no how." Bernice ran her hand across the worn brocaded cushion. "I'm proud for you, li'l sis."

Bernice took five pictures of Earline sitting in the middle of the love seat, beaming, with her newly permed hair and her hands clasped daintily on her knees. Then she took three more with the young'uns sitting up close on the floor in front of her. Earline really wanted a family picture, but Cletis was nowhere to be found, and the truck was gone.

***

He came in much later after they'd all left, Bernice taking Jolene, Little Cletis and Baby Joe off to a church supper over near her own place. Cletis stood steadying himself in the back door. Earline'd seen him out the window, weaving a bit as he walked over from the truck.

She'd frowned, but then put on a cheery face, busying herself in the kitchen.

"Where's everybody got to?" he asked gruffly. His face looked solemn.

"Bernice took 'em, sugar. Took 'em for the whole night. Her church is having a big picnic this evening—lots of other children and all. I'm fixing us up a good dinner here, roast pork and apples, your favorite, and Bernice brought us a banana cream pie, though I really should be giving *her* a pie for the perm she gave me—don't it look nice?" Earline couldn't stop herself talking, though she hadn't really looked him in the face yet.

"Earline, why'd you tell Bernice . . . ."

"I thought we'd have us a nice, quiet dinner, just take our time, and then go in the front room and settle ourselves down on that little love seat to watch Lawrence Welk, or whatever you'd rather…"

"Why'd you make out to Bernice that…"

"That what, dumpling? I just told her that we *found* the love seat. My goodness, ain't that what we did? Now wash up and sit down here at the table while I…"

"You made it sound like we's keeping it. You know you did. It don't belong…"

"Oh, Cletis, it belongs where it belongs. No one ever sits on it in that front parlor at Miz Baptist's. No one ever hardly goes in there. I have to look hard to find what I'm supposed to clean, just lots of old furniture that used to be her mother's and her grandmother's. I don't think she even likes it, seems like it sort of weighs her down. She's hardly ever at home anyway, off traveling or playing bridge, or golf, or tennis. She'll likely be glad to have it off her hands."

Cletis looked doubtful, but he sat down and dug in. They didn't say much during the meal. That was usually all up to Earline anyway; Cletis liked to concentrate on his food. He finished off two platefuls. How he could eat so much and stay so lean was a mystery to Earline.

When he did put down his fork, he looked up at her. "It ain't ours, Earline, it ain't right."

Earline ducked her chin and gave him her puppy look. "Now, sugar, come on, we're just trying it out. I told you Miz Baptist won't be back for a while. And I can always tell Bernice I was fooling her. Here, now, don't be forgetting this," and she handed him a big slice of the pie.

He finished it off and pushed back his chair. "I got to say when it comes to pies, Bernice's is hard to beat."

"Ain't it the truth. I've watched her do it, too, and I still can't come close."

"Don't you fret about that, darlin', ain't many can cook up hog meat like you can, with them apples and gravy and all. You ain't bad with chicken neither."

"Oh, Cletis," she blushed. "You *can* throw a compliment when you take a mind to. Come on, let's just leave this mess here and go sit on that sweet little love seat and watch Lawrence Welk."

Earline settled herself slowly down on the seat. About a third of it was left for Cletis, just enough to snuggle them in cozy.

"Don't you just love those bubbles?" she said as Lawrence Welk began. "They make me feel all giggly like."

"They do?" He looked down at her sideways, then smiled and turned his eyes back to the picture. "I go for the champagne lady myself. She weren't so skinny, I might have to take me a trip out to Hollywood."

"Hush, now, you're just trying to rile me." Earline poked him in the ribs with her elbow and took his hand.

"What you taking hold my hand for, woman? I might need it for something pretty soon."

"Like what, silly?'

"Well, like this," and he reached his free hand down between her full breasts and started nuzzling her neck. Cletis did like to nuzzle, and Earline's plump body offered lots of nuzzling places.

150

"Cletis, don't you want to see the show?"

"I'm seeing it, bean blossom, right here in this sweet little valley." He wiggled his fingers down further.

Earline jerked back and started to giggle. "Stop that, Cletis," she laughed, "you're tickling me silly. Just stop, now."

"I'll stop, sweet pea, I'll stop for sure when I gets down to the bottom."

With that Earline whooped and fell backward against the corner of the love seat in a fit of laughter, pulling Cletis with her. That's when they heard the crack. Before they knew what was happening, Earline was on the floor with Cletis and half the love seat on top of her.

"Oh, Lord, sweet Jesus," wailed Earline. "Oh, help me, Cletis, I think I done broke my back."

Cletis lay over her, wary and stunned, then slowly started extricating himself. "Goddamn, son of a bitch. What kind of fuckin' seat of love is that supposed to be?"

Earline moaned from the floor.

"Hold on, baby, hold on, I'll right you just soon as I get this fuckin' thing off you."

It took some maneuvering for him to get her up, lying there as she was like a full bag of cotton and whimpering every time he tried to hoist her. Finally, he got his hands under her arms and dragged her across the bare floor to the sofa.

"I'm gonna lie down here besides you, Earline, and use my body to push you over on your side. Then maybe with you pulling up and me pushing behind we can get you onto the cushions."

"Alright, sugar," said Earline. She was actually feeling better now that she'd caught her breath, and starting to enjoy Cletis' attention.

"But, honey, just lie here close on the floor besides me a minute, it feels good down here—like that first time in the barn, remember?" And she started to laugh, slow at first and then more and more till her whole soft body was shaking like a vibrating pillow and tears were running out the corners of her eyes. "Too bad," she gasped between fits of laughter, "too bad that Bernice can't, can't...." and she started up again.

"What?" said Cletis, raising up on his elbow and starting to chuckle himself, "too bad what?"

"Too bad," she gasped, "Bernice wasn't here...with her c-c-camera when we..." and they both lay there on the floor shaking and rocking with laughter.

"You feeling better, baby girl?" Cletis asked, sliding his free arm across her middle.

"I sure do, precious. Let's just stay here for a while. The floor feels good, it's not too hard."

"No, it ain't," he rubbed his hand across her tummy. "But something else is." And he slid himself, carefully, over the soft cushion of her body.

RIDING THE PIPPIN

"Well," said Uncle G.L. as he tamped tobacco into his pipe, "in his day, Francis was a hell-raiser. Almost drove Papa crazy."

It was 1947, and we were sitting around Grandmother's living room in Memphis after Uncle Fan's funeral, the grown-ups talking on and on and me getting bored and drowsy, but the "hell" word caught my attention. I'd never heard anyone in Grandmother's family, three sisters and four brothers of which she was the oldest and Francis (my great Uncle Fan) the youngest, use a swear word or even raise a voice. They were reserved people, polite and kindly, but far from colorful.

"What'd he *do*?" I asked. At twelve, I was too old to play with my younger brothers and cousins and too young to join in with the adults, who looked a little uncomfortable to be reminded I was there.

"Oh, just kid stuff," said G.L., waving his hand, "swimming in the river which we were forbidden to do. Papa was deathly afraid of drownings. And smoking fags, coming in late, being a regular Don Juan."

"A what?" I said.

Mother gave me her quit-asking-questions look, and Grandmother cleared her throat and stood up. "Now," she said, "who wants more lemonade?"

I didn't think a lot about it at the time, but from that point on, the enigma of Uncle Fan lay dormant in my mind. How could the "hell-raiser" and the Uncle Fan I knew be the same person?

***

Growing up, I didn't see these great aunts and uncles a lot—we lived in Tipton County, forty miles away—but of them all, Uncle Fan was my favorite. He was as quiet as the rest, soft-spoken, gentle, but, unlike the rest, he had a twinkle in his eye. When he spoke to me or asked to see my dolls, when he read me a book, which he always seemed ready to do, or asked about school or friends, he listened like he really wanted to know. As a child I was full of questions, and I could tell this amused him, but he always took time to respond. He would have enjoyed seeing G.L. trying to explain Don Juan in front of the others.

Uncle Fan didn't have much energy. I recall him at Grandmother's, sitting on the striped porch glider reading the *Saturday Evening Post* and showing me the cartoons. When he got up to go inside, he'd walk slowly, stopping from time to time to take some breaths. He lived in my grandparents' house in the back bedroom; when he wasn't there, he was usually at the VA. "Francis is at the VA again," Grandmother would say to my mother. When I was small, I didn't know what the VA was, and for a long time I thought he worked there. Later I came to understand that was where Uncle Fan went when he wasn't feeling well.

***

Grandmother had been a school teacher. She had lots of story books which I loved and a whole shelf of building blocks, but few toys. What she *did* have though was a small brown leather suitcase, about two feet wide, as I recall, and eight or ten inches deep— just the right size for a child to carry. And inside this suitcase were some very strange things.

Uncle Fan had been a soldier in the war, WWI. He'd gone on a ship across the ocean to France, and when he came home, he brought back what Grandmother called his "kit." Each year she took it into the classroom to show her new group of fourth graders. What was in the kit when he was soldiering, I'll never know, but what was in it when my brothers and I were children, was a green folded army hat that scratched my head when I put it on, a box of rations, a canteen, two rifle shells, a defused hand grenade shaped like a small metal football, and a gas mask.

My brothers fought over the gas mask. When one of them put it over his head, he looked like a giant ant that had grown an elephant's trunk, crinkled like the tube on our old Hoover. I tried the mask on once and felt like I would suffocate. It was hot and dusty. It smelled funny and plastered down my hair.

The ration box was drab green with a waxy feel to it. Everything in it fit tight together, some hard little biscuits, two tins without labels, a small knife, fork, and spoon held together on a ring, a collapsible tin cup, and, to our amazement, a package labeled "powdered eggs." One brother would put on the cap and the gas mask; the other, snap the canteen to his belt. One would hold the two rifle shells, the other the grenade, and they'd play army all through Grandmother's house and yard. Being the oldest, I was the General, the one who said "Forward March" and "Halt."

***

Uncle Fan was a tall thin man, *very* thin. When I sat on his lap to read, I remember the hard seat made by his bony legs. He wore thick gold-rimmed glasses, and his hair was gray and sparse. If I stood behind his chair, I could see the white skin of his scalp. I realize now he would have been in his mid-thirties when I was born in 1934, but he looked like an old man, much older than Grandmother who was fifteen years his senior.

Yet in some ways, he was younger. He noticed things and was curious about them—where the birds' nests were in the yard, what the different flowers were doing, a new ribbon in my hair. And he didn't fuss at us. When my brothers got rowdy and tumbled about, he just sat there with a bemused look while Grandmother put on her stern schoolteacher's face and quickly reprimanded them. His droll comments were never rancorous, and though he mostly stayed in the background, he had a quiet charm and grace, like Fred Astaire with wire rims.

Once when mother was having back problems, I stayed at my grandparents' house for a week or two. I must have been around seven or eight. I was pleased to be going to Memphis instead of out to Aunt Mabel's farm with my brothers, but after a few days, I actually began to miss them. There were no children on Walker Avenue, mostly older folks, and Grandmother kept thinking up ways to amuse me—a trip to the library, a walk to the drugstore for ice cream, collecting lady bugs, lightning bugs, praying mantises for an insect zoo. Schoolteacher that she was, Grandmother always had her day planned, the activities lined up in blocks of time that, after a few days, became boringly predictable.

One late afternoon I was playing a solitary game of jacks on the front porch when Uncle Fan looked up over his newspaper, with its front-page picture of GIs embarking for war, and asked me if I'd ever been to the fairgrounds. The question startled me. I knew about the Memphis Fairgrounds, of course. They were right in the middle of town. Although the Mid-South Fair lasted only two weeks, the amusement park was permanent and stayed opened the full summer season. There was a big billboard out on the highway, and sometimes we drove past the fairgrounds themselves on our way to Grandmother's. The surrounding fence seemed to go on forever, and I could hear music coming from behind the trees that lined the border. Whenever we passed, we begged mother to take us in, but she put us off, saying it was too hot and dusty or too expensive or that we didn't have time. If we raised a clamor, she got annoyed. Mother sighed a lot and read books with beautiful but distressed-looking women on the cover. The words we heard most often were, "Just go on out and play," so I'd never set foot in the fairgrounds.

"No, sir," I said. "Have you?"

"Not for a long, long time." He looked out across the lawn when he said this.

"What's it like?" I asked. "Is it fun?"

"Would you like to go and find out for yourself?"

"Go?" I said. "Do you mean it? When?"

"We could go today if Sister says it's all right."

I was so stunned I just sat there on the concrete porch for a few minutes, holding the small rubber Jack's ball in my hand. Then I scrambled up to ask her. She seemed as surprised as I was. "Francis," she said, coming to the screen door, "why don't we talk about this when Sam gets home. Maybe we could all go another day in the car." There was only one family car, and Uncle Fan never drove, not since the war, mother said.

"We don't need the car," said Uncle Fan. He was smiling, but there was something different in his voice. I'd never heard him disagree with Grandmother about *anything*. "Jennie and I can go on the streetcar. You'd like that, wouldn't you?" He looked in my direction.

"But it's four o'clock. You can't possibly be back in time for dinner." Dinner at Grandmother's was always at six.

"We'll eat something at the fairgrounds, a hot dog maybe and get some lemonade." This was getting better all the time. Uncle Fan stood up as though it had been decided. Grandmother was twisting her hands and looking doubtful. "Fairgrounds food?" she said. "I don't know about that. And you, Francis, are you sure you're up to this? It'll be hot out there, you know."

Uncle Fan reached for his seersucker coat and went inside to get his straw hat. We followed. Grandmother scrubbed my knees and brushed my hair and got out a fresh dress. In no time at all Uncle Fan and I were on the corner waiting for the streetcar to come our way.

***

When we went through the gates of the fairgrounds, I held tight to Uncle Fan's hand. People, all ages, were moving this way and that, hurdy gurdy music was coming from different directions, and loud voices called out to "step right up." I could smell straw and candy apples and popcorn. A clown on stilts with long blue and silver pants walked right past me. I'd never seen so much going on at one time. I pointed to things and jumped up and down. Even when Uncle Fan sat down to rest, as he did from time to time stirring the air with his hat, I couldn't keep still. I rode the prettiest horse on the merry-go-round, shiny black with a bright red halter that had bells, and waved to Uncle Fan as I went around. I ate cotton candy and watched him win a kewpie doll for me at the dart booth. He was smiling the whole time, and his face looked younger by the minute. Then we were standing in front of the Pippin.

I'd never seen or heard of anything like this. The cars went up the hills so slow it seemed they could hardly make it. Then they came flying down with people screaming and laughing and hugging each other before they started up another steep hill. I saw the fun and felt the danger, the thrills and excitement. It was like a foreign country.

159

Uncle Fan looked down at me. "Do you want to go?'

"Go? On the Pippin?" Another car came screeching past. Then a car stopped not far from us, and the people got out. They had big smiles on their faces, and some went right to the ticket booth to buy another ticket.

"Will you go, too?"

"Indeed," he said, and we stepped up to the ticket booth.

Uncle Fan settled us in the front seat and closed the bar across our laps. He put his straw hat between his knees, and we started off. "Hold on," he said.

Up we went and I could see the whole fairground and the people getting smaller. Then I could see the streets beyond the tree-lined fence. Down the first hill I thought my stomach would flip right out. Going up the second, I grabbed the bar as tight as my hands could hold and shut my eyes. And then I started to look forward to the next one. I turned my head to see Uncle Fan. He looked almost like a young man, and he was smiling big. He even laughed, and for the first time in my life, I felt in tune with a grown-up.

I fell asleep in the streetcar on the way home. Uncle Fan woke me up to get off, and we stepped into a warm breezy summer night and walked slowly down the deserted street. There were stars and a half-moon, and I just wanted us to keep walking down Walker Avenue forever.

***

After that Uncle Fan grew frailer. He spent more and more time at the VA and less and less at Grandmother's. When he went there to stay, Mother and I visited him a few times. He'd smile, always glad to see me, but he looked so thin. He was usually in bed or a wheel chair, his voice weak. It was hard for him to talk without coughing.

Uncle Fan lived to see the end of World War II, but he died soon after. A flag lay over his coffin at the funeral home because, said

Grandmother, he had fought for his country. It was hard to imagine my Uncle Fan as a soldier.

***

Some years later when I was in college and old enough to think about such things, Mother and I were looking at some family pictures. By then Grandmother had died and Mother had become the keeper of the family history. "Who's this?" I asked. The photo showed a young man with a wide grin, his straw hat pushed back at a rakish angle, leaning casually against the hood of a Model T. Next to him was a young woman with dark curly hair and a coquettish smile. He must have been looking straight into the Kodak because it seemed like he could step right out of the picture and start talking.

"Why, that's Uncle Fan," she said. "You must remember him."

"Remember him? Of course, I remember him. He was my favorite of all those uncles. But he never looked like this."

"Yes, I know," Mother sighed. "That was before the war, the first war, World War I."

I studied the picture for glimmers of the Uncle Fan I knew. They were there. The smile. The amused look in the eyes. The straw hat. Yet in the photo he looked so healthy, so alive. "What happened to him?"

Mother sighed again, like she was sighing for the whole world. "What happened to him was the war. He was only eighteen when he went. He was gassed."

I had read about that, the gassing in World War I. But after the stories of World War II, the continuous war news I grew up with, the devastation of the atomic bomb, the horrors of the earlier war seemed remote, a made-up story of long ago and far, far away. I remembered as we talked, "Mustard Gas," an article I'd read in *Life* magazine. It penetrated everything—masks, clothes, skin— causing injury and death on the battlefield. Those who survived suffered serious lung damage leaving them disabled the rest of their lives, vulnerable to illnesses such as tuberculosis and pneumonia.

"I was five when he left for the war," said Mother. "He was my favorite uncle, too. He even took me for a ride in that car," she pointed to the photograph, "though I wasn't supposed to tell anybody. When he came back from the war and the hospital, he was a different man. I was eight at the time, and Mama had to send me out of the room because I kept staring at him."

***

Later that week on Grandmother's birthday, Mother and I drove the forty miles to the cemetery to visit her grave. There in the family plot were my great grandparents, my grandparents, Grandmother's older sister, and her three unmarried brothers. That generation was dwindling down. I walked over to Uncle Fan's grave and read the words on his gravestone. They were simple:

Francis Dunavant, 1898-1947
Private
U.S. Army
World War I

At the top of the stone was a small circle with a cross inside, the mark of a serviceman.

***

It was June, a couple of weeks after Memorial Day, and someone, the VFW I suppose, had stuck a little flag on the grave of each veteran. The day was hot and humid, as only Memphis can be, and Uncle Fan's flag hung limp and bedraggled on its little stick.

On the way out of the cemetery we drove past a newly dug grave, open and waiting for the body that would fill it. Several rows of chairs stood on one side and on the other stood a tall, shiny American flag beside a bright array of flowers.

***

"Another soldier," said my mother. She took a sharp breath that sounded almost like a sob, but when I looked, her hands were tight on the steering wheel and her face set and stony. "Korea this time." She said. My brothers were thirteen and fourteen.

JAPANESE FAN

Avis lies in bed listening to the early morning rain and thinking of all the different places she has lived in her ninety years. More than she can count. Last night she dreamed of her mother, who had lived in the same house her whole life, the family home in rural Virginia where she was born and where she raised her family. The idea of living anywhere else had never occurred to her. When she died, the household accumulations of several generations were astounding.

Over the last few weeks Avis has once again been preparing to move, a process she knows so well—emptying drawers, sorting contents, deciding what to keep, what to let go. Now she's almost finished, just a few items left in the Malaysian teak chest, things still wrapped in tissue from her last move. She sighs and shakes her head. How odd that she, always a morning person, often a predawn riser, is lying in bed daydreaming. A slight heaviness—is it the rainy atmosphere?—seems to be keeping her here. Ah, well, time to get on with it. She pushes back the covers and reaches for her old chenille robe. It's almost day.

***

In the living room Avis runs her hand over the familiar carvings that decorate the chest—elephants, fish, birds, and flowers. Despite its impractical size for her new and smaller living space, she's taking it along. Even if her eyesight fails completely, the eyes of her fingers will bring it into view.

She opens the lid and removes the last items, each carefully labeled and already designated for its new owner. One by one she places them in the right pile and gathers up the extra packing paper crumpled in the bottom. With difficulty she rises. "Old bones," her mother used to say. As she turns towards the trash bag, something falls on her slippered foot. Curious, she places a hand on the chest to steady herself and slides her fingers across the floor beneath her bathrobe. What could it be? Nothing is missing. Her hand closes on a smooth object, wood of some kind, and she raises it up. A fan, of all things. A Japanese fan. Probably hidden in the bottom of this chest for years, traveling with them from place to place as they moved.

167

Releasing the tiny catch, she spreads open the fan. A delicate branch of cherry blossoms sweeps up and across its fluted surface, the beauty of a long-ago tree captured on rice paper. In the soft gray light of early morning she recalls the fan, though she hasn't seen it for years. And she remembers herself as a young woman, still a girl really, though married, who paused at a street stall and then, on a whim, bought it.

***

Tomorrow Avis is moving to a one-bedroom efficiency apartment in Assisted Living, a transition she thinks of as the last stage of a long winnowing process. With Malcolm she'd lived the interesting life of a state department wife, residing in numerous countries, meeting people others only read about, hostessing countless diplomatic dinners. She has served eel soup to forty guests, can say "How very nice to meet you" in six languages. But she was green at the beginning, no doubt about it. The skills required of her had been consciously cultivated, not an easy task for one of her impulsive nature.

In their first posting, at the end of what had seemed to her a thrilling and highly successful evening, Malcolm, fifteen years her senior, had patted her hand on the way home. "Now, my dear," he said, not unkindly, "you must keep in mind that in all situations we represent our country. All eyes notice our gestures, our expressions, our remarks, some of yours which, while charming in one so young, may lack the dignity of our position."

It had taken her aback and reminded her of a comment her mother had made years earlier when she was chastised at school for her "deportment"—talking too much in class, asking "why" too often. And when, during art class, she had drawn her *own* picture, a view of the mountains seen from her desk, rather than copying the dull house-with-picket-fence assigned to them in the drawing book. "Avis," her mother had said, "you *must* show respect for your teachers by doing as you are told. And keep in mind, dear, that in public you represent our family."

"But why must I keep that in mind?" she'd asked. "Why can't I just be Avis?" Her mother had laughed. "Well, let us hope as you mature, you find the answer to that question."

Avis had not put this question to Malcolm. An able diplomat, he was of a serious nature; first and last, he must remain dignified. It came naturally to him, what she teasingly called his "Boston bearing." Not that he was what one would call *stiff*, not really with his quick, wry humor and attentive expression.. But his voice was always measured, always reasonable. It seemed *she* was always trying to measure up, at least outwardly, not wanting to cause him distress, though the protocols and formalities of the diplomatic corps amused her—like a game of pretend that they all deemed so important.

***

She was eighteen when they met at her aunt's in Washington all those years ago. "Come meet my college roommate," Cousin Reg had motioned to her, "the smartest junior diplomat in the corps."

"Reg is an incurable exaggerator," said Malcolm smiling.

"Only when it's true, or at least probable. And this bright little bird is my country cousin Avis, who has an incurable yen to travel."

They had made a good pair, a "good team," as Malcolm said. People thought they complimented each other.

Years of different postings, primarily in the Far East as Malcolm was fluent in Oriental languages, allowed them to live in many interesting places, collect many beautiful things—paintings and wall hangings, delicately carved screens, exquisite ivory figures, statues of various eras, ancient bowls of china and clay. They chose them with the care and enthusiasm they might have lavished on children which, for some reason, never came. Avis regretted this. She was quite at ease with children, would have enjoyed a houseful. But Malcolm assured her it was just as well they'd had none, considering the frequency of their moves. And she had observed herself that most state department families sent their children off to private school at an early age. She would have hated that. Instead their spacious overseas quarters were filled with the works of artists and craftsmen from other cultures, some more ancient than she could imagine.

Her eyes fall now on a Chinese scroll hanging between the two windows, the spare and defining brush strokes of mountains caught momentarily in morning mist. After all these years, she still wonders how it's possible to achieve something so immediate yet so eternal. Malcolm knew it was a valuable find. He could have been a museum director with his eye for authenticity. She smiles to recall how much he enjoyed exercising his taste and acuity, separating "wheat from chaff," cataloguing each item.

He had not wanted to buy the Malaysian chest. An inferior piece, he'd said, obviously worked on by a number of different carvers and overpriced for those who could not tell the difference. Yes, she could see his point; she could understand the wisdom of his hesitation. Definitely not a treasure. But she loved it on sight, just the right size for her sitting room, and surely they could bargain for it. She didn't tell him that one of the things she loved most about the chest was the very fact that different hands *had* worked on it, perhaps over a period of time— an unconscious collaboration that moved her. She took delight in connecting with those artists, imagining their concentration and vision as moment by moment they carved their creation.

She lifts a statue from the coffee table, a kneeling old man, his aged Japanese face deeply lined. How does his humble posture, his plain robe and kind smile manage to convey such strength and wisdom? A sage, timeless yet present. A six-inch block of wood transformed by the carver's hands long ago and held today in her own. A current of joy runs up her spine.

***

In retirement, they had built a house around these treasures, enjoying each beautiful object and the memory of where they had found it. After Malcolm's death, she took comfort in those shared memories the objects evoked. But, in time, she often could not remember the details surrounding a piece and had to look them up in Malcolm's careful notations. And their very preciousness became heavy, as though the full burden of appreciation was more than she could carry alone, as though they should be shared, seen, enjoyed by others.

170

The house also felt like more than she wanted to manage, and there followed a series of smaller spaces—a lovely pink cottage, a seaside condo, her retirement community apartment with its mountain view. The lightness of spirit she felt with each intuitive move was beautifully freeing.

Of course, with each of these moves the collection had to become smaller, too, and though it took time and consideration, it was less difficult than she had imagined. She found new homes for the objects where they would be valued—small museums and private collections. Or close friends who appreciated their loveliness. She developed her own little ritual for saying goodbye, holding or touching each piece, taking it in, connecting once more with its beauty. Then she released them like captured butterflies let loose into the world. And each time she delighted anew in those she kept, the ones that most touched *her.*

In the years since Malcolm's death she has come to realize how much she *likes* moving. Being settled forever in one place never held much appeal for her. Now she is culling her collection for the last time. Is it this that is dampening her spirits?

She looks down at the fan and slowly opens and closes it. How light and airy it is, not meant to last forever like the ivories, but to stir the air of the moment with its delicate beauty. She still remembers the correct way to do this, the language of the fan. A sweet musty aroma from the sandalwood spokes wafts upward.

What a remarkable thing that she was once a girl. That she knew how to stir hearts with the flick of a painted fan, looking over its curved rim with her large dark eyes or spreading its delicate blossoms across the bosom of her gown. She smiles at this secret reverie. Had Malcolm ever noticed this fan she had somehow held on to? It was not the kind of thing he would remember.

But isn't life itself a collection, she muses, one of moments, many as clear and luminous as beads on a string? Yet she doesn't want to live in the past, in the scrapbook of her life. A butterfly collection,

171

however interesting, is never like watching a butterfly move through the air, feeling the flutter of its wings in your breast.

"Bright little bird" her cousin Reg used to call her—flashing her feathers, laughing, and darting about. What is she now—a seagull, perhaps, riding the winds, taking in the broader view. Yet all of it is there inside her, all coalescing in this very moment. She thinks of her new room, its nice window where she will see sky and mountains—and other birds, even from her bed. In its own way, this too will be an adventure.

She moves the fan lightly through the air, following the path of a butterfly. Then she catches sight of herself in the sliding glass door and laughs at her own absurdity—a gaunt old woman in bathrobe and slippers, unruly strands of gray hair hanging down from the twist of her bun. Still, in the dim morning reflection, she might at a glance appear differently. Turning her body slightly so that the image looks back at her over one shoulder, she flicks open the fan with a quick graceful motion of her wrist, raises the flowering cherry branch to her face, and flutters it beneath her eyes.

BYRON PATE

Byron Pate was a slim, lightweight boy with no distinguishing features. He slipped though the hallways unnoticed, head slanted, eyes on the floor, his whole body in a permanent lean. With hair the shade of whey and almost translucent skin, he appeared and disappeared from a room like an apparition.

Byron always sat in the far-left corner of every classroom near one of the two hall doors. He would slip in unnoticed and sit with his head hung over his notebook while the rest of us walked in, talking and laughing until the last bell. He would slip out as soon as we were dismissed and slide through the halls before they got crowded to be in the far-left seat of his next class, head over notebook, when most of us arrived.

He *never* raised his hand, never volunteered to go to the blackboard. Once a substitute teacher called on him for an answer. We all looked back to see his face turn purple and his eyes turn into long startled ovals like a comic book character. He shook his head in the slightest motion as I quickly raised my hand, and the sub, after a moment of puzzlement, moved on.

Because I had begun to notice him, I seemed to see him everywhere. I think I was fascinated by how invisible he was, how removed from the consciousness of most students. And the fact that he had managed to do that in the midst of a small-town middle school bustling with kids! One night, as Mother was cooking supper, and I was cracking eggs for an omelet, I asked her about the Pates. Actually, I asked if Byron was an *albino* (having just become familiar with the word.). She looked surprised and stopped stirring the soup.

"An albino? Where did you get that idea? I don't think so . . ." her voice trailed off. "Well, maybe, but I don't think so. Why do you ask?"

"Oh, he's just always so *pale,* pale and watery as . . . as an egg-white. I just wondered about him?"

"Hmm . . . I see him sitting with his mother in church, but I don't think he goes to Sunday School, does he? She's pretty protective of him."

Why? I wondered. Why does she need to protect him?

I noticed, then, that she always had her hand lightly on his arm or shoulder as they walked in and out of church, as though she were guiding or being guided by Byron. Well, I thought, maybe albinos have weak eyes. His eyes were kind of pink-rimmed and rabbity.

My grandmother made most of my clothes on her new electric sewing machine, but she didn't do any "close work." For embroidery, lace, cross-stitching, etc., she went to Mrs. Pate who was known for her skill with fine detail. One day Grandma said she was going over to Mrs. Pate's to get some smocking done on a baby dress, and I asked to come along. She hesitated, then said,

"Well, alright, if you can promise to be quiet and not ask questions. Mrs. Pate has *nerves,* you know, she needs peace and quiet."

I *didn't* know. And what was so special about Mrs. Pate's nerves? I thought everyone had them. But I wanted to go, to see what their upstairs apartment looked like, to see Byron in it, so I didn't ask. Grandma was always ready to answer my questions, but when she got that look on her face, kind of frowning and purse-mouthed, and put her stiff leather pocketbook over her arm, it was best to be quiet.

Mrs. Pate and Byron lived in an upstairs apartment in one of the older houses on Church Street. As we climbed the outside steps, Grandma huffing and puffing a bit, I was surprised to see that we were half-hidden by the leaves of an old maple tree. One could sit on these steps in summertime, look up and down the street, and never be seen. How cool!

I was a secret "watcher" myself, as far back as I could remember. I had learned at an early age that if I slipped into the grown-folks dining room for the large family dinners we had every Sunday, and scooted under the dark oak table with its big center pedestal, and nestled between two of its lion's-paw feet, I could hear all the grownups conversation, their jokes and gossip, and stories. Grandpa was a great drawling story-teller, going back to horse and buggy days when he was a boy—the tricks and troubles he and his brothers got into—that Halloween night back in ought-four when, *somehow,* a mule got into the 2nd floor study hall of the high school, or the time Miss Willie Flippen's horse got spooked and ran off with her in the buggy all the way down Main Street and out the Mason Road with half the town and all the dogs chasing and barking after it.

I could picture Byron sitting quietly on these steps, watching people coming and going, his secret view of the world.

When Mrs. Pate opened the door, we walked into a sparsely furnished, darkish room—shades pulled half down, floor of brown linoleum. A small table sat in one corner with two straight-backed chairs. A privacy screen for women to try on their dresses stood in another corner. The rest of the room was devoted to sewing—what looked like an antique treadle machine with wide wrought-iron legs and dark wooden casing, a three-level wicker stand like Grandma's, half-opened, measuring tape hanging out, pins and needles stuck in a red cat-shaped cushion, scissors, pinking shears, and stacks of different-colored spools of thread.

While Grandma and Mrs. Pate talked about the baby dress, I sat on one of the straight-back chairs and looked around the room. There were no newspapers or magazines, games or books, plants, animals or even fish. I could see a short hallway to the left with two doors leading, I assumed, to bedroom and bath. Mrs. Pate was wearing a freshly-ironed, but faded blue housedress, beige lisle stockings, and worn embroidered slippers. Her mousy-blonde hair was rolled at the neck and secured with hair pins. I had never seen her without a hat. She was quiet and deferential towards Grandma, eyes cast down, head slowly nodding. Byron was nowhere in sight.

"Where is Byron's daddy?" I asked as we drove home. "Did he die or something?"

"We don't know," said Grandma. "She moved here with Byron a couple of years ago. No one knows much about her— except her skill with a needle."

They were a mystery and so unknown and different that my curiosity peaked. In a town where *everyone* knew *everybody*, going back for generations, here was a woman and her child about whom everyone knew *nothing*. My Nancy Drew persona switched into gear. There must be a story here. Were they hiding out from someone? Had they run away from danger, from their family, from fear? I was intrigued.

***

Our school cafeteria, noisy, low-ceiling and spread out, was dominated by the team guys—football, basketball, soccer. I hated carrying my tray past them to get to a quieter spot on the edge where I usually sat with a small group of friends. The jocks would joke and jostle, call out to the girls who passed by or anyone they could embarrass. Worst of all was when they joined voices for a cheer or a cat-calling joke on someone.

One day, as Byron was sitting by himself at a far table, head hanging over his plate, I heard the rhythm of a favorite chant flying louder and louder through the air.

> *Byron Pate, if you are able,*
> *take your elbows off the table.*

I took a quick look Byron's way. He was so deep into his own world, I thought maybe he hadn't heard them. When he didn't respond in any way, I hoped their focus would turn to someone else. But no. They only grew louder, more persistent.

> *Byron Pate, if you are able,*
> *take your elbows off the table.*
> *Byron Pate, if you are able,*
> *take your elbows off the table.*
> *Byron Pate, if you are able,*
> *take your elbows off the table.*

I saw Byron's head sink lower towards his plate as his skin turned from pink, to scarlet. My heart was beating fast. I felt his embarrassment, along with my own frustration and growing anger at my inability to stop them. But what could I do? Finally, the bell rang and, with much scraping of chairs, students hurried off to their fourth-period classes. The next day, I went through the food line, picked up my tray and walked straight to Byron's table.

The cafeteria was a dimly-lit basement room with high narrow windows and oblong wooden tables that seated six students. Byron always sat on the far side in the last place so I sat down on the opposite side at the other end. I could tell he was startled as his head sank so low I was afraid it would land on his mashed potatoes. I couldn't think of a single thing to say about my strange intrusion, but the two of us eating at the same table and not saying a word seemed ridiculous. Finally, as I grew more and more self-conscious, I blurted out, "Byron, could you slide the salt my way?"

He managed to do this without looking up, so I quickly added, "How's the meatloaf?"

He gave me a blank look, then looked down at his plate as though surprised to find it still there. "Err, O.K.," he mumbled. Then the first bell rang, and he dug in without another word.

I was not surprised by his reluctance to respond, but I *was* surprised by my own reaction. I felt strangely energized, uplifted. I had made a small step in my project to uncover the mystery of Byron Pate.

***

That year I had started taking organ lessons from my long-time piano teacher. Because the church was often in use after school, my lesson was scheduled for 7 am every Wednesday morning—and twice a week I could use the same time for practice.

I loved my early morning walks up to the church. The air was fresh, every blade of grass was sparkling with dew, birds were waking up, calling and cooing, and the whole rest of the town was still asleep. I was the only one there to hear them. I'd walk up the worn steps of the red brick building, push open the big oak door and step into the sanctuary. Its vaulted bead-and-board ceiling, the shafts of sunlight shining through the stained-glass windows, the curved wooden pews, and the rich wine-colored carpet always filled me with awe.

I'd pass the communion rail, climb the few steps to the choir loft, and stand in front of the magnificent brass pipes of the organ. Then I'd hoist my small frame onto the bench and wait for my teacher to arrive.

During that time, I ran my fingers across the silent keys, feet skidding from pedal to wooden pedal, and imagined a glorious sound filling the air behind me. When Miss Ermine appeared, quietly and kindly as always, she would nod with her half-smile and say, "Now let's practice our scales."

That part I had mastered on the piano and found my way across the organ keys fairly easily, but when it was time to play my assigned piece for that week, my hands started to perspire. When the right chords are played on the organ, glorious music fills the air, as though an entire symphony is playing. But when the wrong notes are hit, a screeching sound fills the sanctuary like a hundred fingernails scraping across a blackboard.

A tilted mirror was placed above the organ to allow the organist a view of the congregation, especially useful for weddings, funerals, and processionals. I was playing my recital piece one day when I thought I saw a slight movement in the last row of the church. But when I looked again, it was gone. Probably a trick of light, I surmised, and continued my playing. When it was over, Miss Ermine leaned in to make a mark on the score, and I glanced in the mirror again. The door to the back vestibule was swinging closed.

When I left the church that morning, I stood on the top step and looked across the street towards the Pate's apartment. The top few steps hidden by the maple tree branches were directly in my line of vision. I mulled this over all the way up College Street to school. It gave me a funny feeling. For one thing, I was enjoying secretly spying on Byron, but I wasn't sure how I felt about it if *he* was spying on *me*. It seemed kind of spooky. Not that I was afraid of him or anything. He was only a lonely, timid boy. I guess I just wanted to help him be more normal, feel more comfortable with himself. But all the way up the hill, I kept glancing over my shoulder.

I didn't sit at Byron's table that day or for the rest of the week. I sat with my friends, my back to Byron, and tried to forget he was there. I was still curious about him, but I wanted to pursue that on my own terms. Therefore, I was totally surprised when the doorbell rang on Saturday morning, and there was Byron holding a package wrapped in brown paper.

"Oh," I said, "is this for Grandma?" I stupidly asked.

"For Mrs. Fisher," he whispered, looking down at the floor.

"I'll get her," I answered, but as I turned the sound of his strained voice stopped me.

"Do you have a piano?"

He was looking into the house with such urgency in his voice, I was almost too startled to speak.

"Well, It's my grandmother's. I mean, we live with her. It's in the dining room. . . though it's cold in there. . .They close it off in the winter. . ."

"Can...can I see it?" he asked, his eyes turning into ovals again.

"See it? Well, sure—I guess so. Why not?"

We walked through the living room, which was also unheated in winter, and stood awkwardly in front of the black upright. I opened the lid, and we looked down together at the yellowing keys, Byron with an expression of awe. I realized I had never looked at them that way. The piano was just something that had always been in the dining room which I entered to practice my pieces every day or two. I had never seen it as special, a thing of wonder.

"It's beautiful," said Byron. "How did you get it?"

"Oh, we've always had it. I mean, it belonged to Grandma when she was young. She loved to play. They even sent her to a conservatory

181

in Memphis for a year, before she married Grandpa. He says she could have given concerts if she'd stayed, but she married him instead. Now she only plays for the Beethoven Club sometimes. They meet each month and play pieces for each other."

His pale eyelashes fluttered rapidly, and his face actually colored.

"Can I touch it?" he whispered.

That night at supper Grandma said, "I had the most unexpected phone call today from Mrs. Pate. She's making curtains for Ermine McNeely in exchange for piano lessons for Byron, and she's wondering if he could practice on *our* piano in exchange for some sewing work."

We sat there a little stunned, trying to take that odd notion in— the pros (charitable) and cons (disruptive) and trying to imagine the weirdness of it, vis a vis our household routine.

"Well," said Grandpa, "I admire her intention, willing to work extra to help her boy, and I'm out of the house most of the day anyway so it won't affect me. I think the rest of you have to decide."

Mother and Grandma looked at each other. We lived upstairs, so mother saw no objection. "It's up to you, Miss Nellie," she said. "After all, it's your piano."

I could see Grandma didn't want it to be up to her. "I suppose it's the Christian thing to do." She sighed and turned to me. "How do you feel about it, honey?"

I wasn't at all sure *how* I felt about it. Byron Pate coming to *our* house. Regularly!

How would that feel? What would my friends say? Would I have to hear him practice? Would I want to? And how would it affect *my* practice time? I saw Mother looking hard at me, frowning at my hesitation.

"Sure," I said. "Whatever you all think." And I asked to be excused from the table.

So that's how it happened. Byron came straight from school Monday, Wednesday, and Friday and practiced for an hour. I walked home with a friend or stayed after school to help the librarian. For some reason, I didn't want to pass him coming out of my house. And I hated it when Grandma spoke about his *progress. Such nimble piano sounds! Such rapid improvement!*

"Well," said Grandpa one day at dinner. "How's the piano boy doing?"

'O.K., I guess," I answered. "I'm not really here when he's practicing."

"He's diligent," said Grandma, "and punctual. He even likes to play his scales!"

She gave me an admonishing look, which I chose to ignore. Scales were boring—boring to play and boring to hear—over and over and over. I was a slow sight-reader, too. But I worked hard to memorize a piece as soon as I could. It was *then* that I began to enjoy the playing. Once memorized, I could start to own it, hear it over and over in my head, express the emotion I felt in it, feel myself connecting with the composer.

One day when I came home from school, I heard the beautiful music of Chopin coming from the dining room. I froze. Surely Byron had not progressed that much! And it wasn't even his day to practice! I walked back to the breakfast room and pushed open the swinging door to peek inside. It was Grandma! I hadn't heard her play in a long time, and it was beautiful. Even from the back of the room I could tell by the way her shoulders swayed from side to side that she was smiling. When she finished the waltz, she sat there in reverie, looking out the window.

"That was beautiful, Grandma," I said, startling her a bit. "I never heard you play that before."

"Just practicing. Annie Hamilton and I are playing for the Beethoven Club on Saturday. You might like to come. It's wonderful how the notes resound in that high-ceiling parlor of the Community House. And you wouldn't have to stay for the whole meeting."

***

The Community House was a big, old Victorian House across from the Presbyterian Church. It was built by Major Dunlap when he returned from the Confederate Army and, at the time, was considered the finest house in town. When he died, he left it to the town for "community use." And all these years later, it was still well-used. The Major's library room became the town's public library, the parlor with its two Baby Grand pianos became a reception and performance space, and up the gracious staircase were the Boy Scout room, the Girl Scout room, and a room for the Red Cross where my mother and grandmother and other ladies rolled bandages and knitted sox for soldiers during World War II.

I was looking forward to the concert, to seeing Grandma play on that beautiful piano with its lid raised like a great black wing—until she looked up from her sewing and said, "Byron wants to come, too. I mentioned it to him today after his practice, and he said 'Yes, ma'am,' right away. I don't think the poor boy gets to go much of anywhere, his mother not having a car, you know."

I sighed, but I knew she was right about Byron. Luckily, their apartment was only a short block from the Community House, so we wouldn't have to pick him up. I couldn't imagine being in the back seat with Byron!

The day of the concert came. Grandma told me to wear something nice, *not* my usual Saturday clothes, and I noticed she was wearing her best dress, lilac blue with pearl buttons.

Even Grandpa had on a dress shirt and had shined his shoes, when just a few hours earlier he was wearing overalls and work boots and digging in the garden.

I was surprised to see that Grandma, who was always calm and unruffled, was a little nervous. She kept taking her best lace-trimmed handkerchief out of the bosom of her dress and patting her neck. She walked into the dining room to get her music off the piano, then set it

184

down somewhere else, and we all had to scurry around to find where she had put it.

Finally, we got in the car and drove off.

Byron had his pale hair slicked down to one side, and with his wheat-colored sports coat and wire-rimmed glasses, he looked like a wizened little old man. Grandma had saved places for us in the middle of the front row, but I was not about to sit there with Byron, in front of everybody. I nudged him and pointed to the last two seats on the end where we could make a quick escape through the kitchen when the music ended.

At last, after much bustling and settling in, the Beethoven Club president rose to announce the pieces, and a great hush settled over the room.

"Nellie Fisher and Annie Hamilton will play a two-piano arrangement of the Polonaise by Frederick Chopin."

The two women raised their relaxed wrists, paused for a second, and then attacked the pianos. I felt Byron startle with the first loud chords, but then, I was so filled with the rippling beauty of the music, the richness of the chords, and the bitter-sweet melody, I was transported to another realm. The only thing that kept me grounded was the movement of Grandma's arms and shoulders, left and right, forward and back, in perfect flowing rhythm with the music.

I knew her pillowy shoulders, her ample bosom. Since I was a baby, and even as a young girl, when I was hurt or sad or unable to sleep, she was the one who took me into her lap and rocked me over and over, hundreds of miles I'd guess, on her sheltering breast. Here, at the piano, her whole body was playing the music. At one point she raised her head and seemed to look off in the distance with a dreamy, half-smiling expression, and I saw Nellie, the girl in her wedding photo, with the eighteen-inch waist and upswept hair, looking fondly into her new husband's eyes.

Then, suddenly, it was over. I had to elbow Byron twice to get his attention. His chin was dropped, and actual tears were running down

185

his cheeks. Everyone was clapping and clapping. "Byron," I said loudly, "move." And we slipped out of the room, through the swinging doors, and into the pantry.

I had been in this house many times—recitals, birthday parties, even for tap-dancing lessons—but for Byron it was all new.

"Do you want to see the rest of the house?" I asked, not really knowing what to do with him.

"O.K." he said, blinking his eyes and looking up at the high kitchen ceiling.

I was feeling a little mischievous after all the emotion of the music and pointed to a tall closed door. "That goes to the cellar," I whispered. "They keep it locked, but I know where they keep the key. Want to go exploring?"

Without waiting for an answer, I reached to the back of a drawer that held tea towels, pulled out an old-fashioned key on a fraying string, and pushed it in the lock.

Byron looked alarmed. "Do you think we should do this?" he whispered as we heard the lock click open.

But I had already turned the doorknob, the door opened wide, and we were staring into dark nothingness.

"There's a flashlight in the pantry," I said, waving him towards it. When he returned we stepped inside, and I pulled closed the door. The flashlight beamed on steep dusty steps and murky darkness. In the dim glow Byron looked more like a ghost than ever. We had entered another world.

As our eyes adjusted to the darkness, we started slowly down the steep steps. I kept my right hand on the rough stone wall for balance as the musty stench of mildew filled my nose. A spider web swept across my face. I heard Byron suck in air as something with a tail scurried through the shadows below. Without a word we both turned and climbed back up the steps.

"We can come back another day," I said, "with two flashlights. Let's go upstairs, and I'll show you the other rooms." Byron looked relieved, and we started up the beautiful winding staircase to the second-floor gallery, a wide spacious hall with tall windows at each end.

I showed him the door to the Girl Scout room, the Boy Scout room, the room for the Red Cross. Of course, they were all locked. Byron seemed intrigued with the large verdigris doorknobs and kept trying them, even though he knew they wouldn't open. He said he liked the feel of them in his hand.

Off to the right at the far end of the hall was a rectangular room with windows along the entire back wall. There was no furniture, just a couple of long built-in chests under the windows and some dusty boxes. But it was sunny, and we could see over the lawn to rooftops of houses on the next street. After the dungeon atmosphere below, it was delightfully bright and cheerful, and I imagined being a bird and flying out the window and up into the blue sky. It was then I saw the small window latches.

"Look at these fasteners, Byron. Do you think that's how they let in the air?"

He tried to jiggle one and then another. His fingers were long and slender, piano fingers, I thought, and they seemed to work deftly as he explored each little latch.

"Rusted tight," he said, "but if I work on them . . . ." I could see he wanted to do it. I had no patience with things like that, but he actually looked intrigued!

"Yoo-hoo," Grandma called up the stairs. "Time to go, children. We have to lock up."

We headed towards the stairs with its curved dark wood banister. If only I had on my jeans, I thought, instead of this Sunday dress! I was dying to slide down that banister.

***

A week or so later, when I left the church after practice, I found an intricately folded-up note in my bicycle basket: *Saturday 1 o'clock.* It was written in Byron's spidery handwriting, and I knew he meant the window-room. The front door to the Community House would be open for the Library, but no other activities were planned for that day.

We pushed open the big door and slipped quietly past the Library room whose door was always closed to protect the books. Then we tip-toed up the steps to our newly discovered sunroom. The day was perfect—mild, but not too hot, blue sky with a few lazy white clouds, a light breeze. Byron started to throw open the windows without even a squeak!

"How did you do it?" I asked as I looked at brass latches that had been rusty and unyielding the week before. He smiled an impish little smile and slowly pulled a carpenter's file from his bookbag.

"Where on earth did you get that?"

"From our landlady's shed," he whispered, "where she keeps the old lawn-mower I use to cut the grass every week. I was sharpening the blades when I got the idea."

"But didn't anybody hear you," I asked, thinking of all the people that went in and out of the House.

"Nope," he grinned shyly, "And I used it to work open a kitchen window, the one behind that big hydrangea bush. Nobody ever knew I was there. I'd ride my bike over after supper, work on them for a while, and get home before dark. Once I figured out how to do the first one, it was pretty easy."

I looked at the nails of his white slender fingers. They were immaculate as ever. How in the world had he cleaned off all that rust? I was about to ask when he unlatched the window closest to us and said, "Come look. See how the lower roof is right under this window? I can step out on it!" and he swung one leg over and straddled the sill.

"Byron! Stop!" I called out. "You're scaring me."

188

"It's OK," he said, climbing back in. "I tried it the other day. The slope is gentle and my feet never slipped once. When you get to the top of it, there's a big flat space right in the middle of the roof—like a terrace or something, where we can sit and look down on the town without *anybody* seeing us!"

I leaned cautiously out the window and looked up. This must be the roof that topped a part of the kitchen that had been added on when the building was "modernized" years ago.

Byron was right; it had a gentle slope that led up to a higher gable. I was intrigued. Being small for my age and skinny, I had never been considered athletic. Most of my friends were on some team or other—basketball, softball, gymnastics—but my arms were so weak that, even as a young child, I could never turn a proper cartwheel. Instead of legs whirling up in the air, my butt stayed midway to the ground, and I ended up looking like a kicking donkey.

But I had always loved to climb, loved looking out from high places—the apple trees in Grandpa's small orchard, the hay loft in the barn where I could look across the alley into our neighbors' back yards, the tall pecan tree in our side yard where I would climb to eye level with our upstairs kitchen and wave at my alarmed mother.

I really wanted to be up on that rooftop, wanted it badly, but could I trust my legs and arms to get me there?

"Just watch how I do it," urged Byron. "Follow me."

"Well," I said to Byron, "O.K., I'll try, but go slow."

He was nimble. He climbed easily over the sill and, leaning forward like a spider, walked his thin arms and legs up the roof and sat on the flat top. I followed his lead, staying as close to the side of the sunroom as possible. My sneakers were new and held the shingles easily.

"Good," said Byron. "Don't look back. Just keep coming forward."

189

In no time at all I was over the peak and sitting on the flat surface. It was glorious!

Byron and I looked at each other and laughed. He pointed to the Presbyterian church across the street. Even though it was on a small rise, we were eye-level with it! Toward the north, we could see the cupola on top of the County Courthouse, and west of us was the train depot, steel tracks shining in the afternoon sun.

Few people were about this time of day, and they looked so *small*—like children in grown-up clothes. We only recognized Mr. Bringle because of his cane and his Panama hat.

Joey Marshall, delivering the afternoon paper, looked like he was riding a tricycle. The cars looked like toys.

Then I lay back on the roof and watched a few puffs of clouds move lazily across the bright blue sky. If only I could stay here forever.

I must have dozed off because Byron sneezed, and I woke up with a start. The clouds had turned smudgy and shadowed the sun.

"We better go down," said Byron. "It's getting towards supper time."

I stood up, stretched, and walked over to the peak of our lower roof. We both sat, and then it hit me. We had to go *down*. Our *feet* had to go first! On our bellies, we wouldn't be able to see where we were going!

"Byron," I said, "I can't do this. There's nothing to hold on to!"

"It's not hard. Just watch—I'll show you."

He made a move to go down.

"Wait," I screamed, panic starting to set in. "Don't leave me up here by myself!"

Byron looked totally flummoxed. "But ... but ... but," he stammered. "We can't *stay* here. We *have* to go down. I mean, night will come. . .and that cloud passing over the sun. . .it might rain on us, the shingles get slick!"

190

I knew he was right. Even if we yelled for help at the top of our voices, no one would hear us. Even if they did and called the fire department, everyone in town would come out and gawk at us. That was a worse thought than staying here all night!

"Look," he said, in a rather grown-up way that surprised me, "I'll go down and get help. I've done it before, it was O.K. You just sit tight here and wait for us."

I took a deep breath, and then another. Byron's voice was so sensible.

"O.K.," I said, "let me see how *you* do it. Then coach me from the window after you get in."

I watched him sit on the roof with his legs bent and his sneakers flat on the shingles. He leaned backwards, his hands flat down on the roof, his body right next to the wall. Then he inched down towards the window, grabbed the sill, and hauled his body through.

It *did* look pretty easy. "Keep looking at the wall," he said. "Don't look down."

I scooted down at a much slower pace, inch by inch, but I kept going. Soon he was helping me through the window. I stood perfectly still for a minute or two. The old wooden floor felt wonderfully solid beneath my feet.

***

Things changed between Byron and me after that—not on the surface so much, we didn't become best buddies, spend lots of time together, or anything like that. But we had a new regard for each other, a trust and a secret, a mutual adventure that we would never tell—not to our families who would be terribly upset and give us all kinds of grief, or our classmates. Although it might have earned us some teenage admiration, they might be challenged to try it themselves—with a more disastrous ending.

I continued my early morning organ lessons; Byron continued his practice on Grandma's piano. He really was good. Sometimes I would climb the tall pecan tree, which was right outside the dining room window, and listen to him play. At Miss Ermine's suggestion, he had begun organ lessons also, and I was amazed how quickly he seemed at home with it.

***

In the middle of our junior year, Mrs. Pate suffered a stroke. I couldn't quite take it in. No one in my family had ever died or had a serious illness. She was taken to a nursing home in Memphis, and Byron was taken in by the minister's family who lived next door to the church.

They had a piano in their home, and he was allowed to play the church organ whenever it wasn't being used. Sometimes I would ride my bicycle up to the church after school and sit in one of the pews just to listen. He played better than I could after four years of lessons.

But it was more than that. There was such feeling in his playing as it filled the empty sanctuary.

***

Mrs. Pate died in early spring. In May we graduated. I got a scholarship to a small church college in Virginia, and Byron left for a Music Conservatory in Nashville. I learned later that Grandma had spearheaded a drive to collect enough money to send him the first year.

After that, the school gladly offered him free admittance.

My college had a small music department, and I signed up for Dr. Bremen's Music Appreciation class. He was a great pianist and had a full library of orchestral recordings. We learned to listen more deeply, to appreciate more fully, to identify theme & variation, change in key, the effect of composers' directions like *adagio, pianissimo, forte.* I always looked forward to his classes.

But I never took another lesson in piano or organ. I realized that, despite Grandma's dreams for me where music was concerned, no matter how much I practiced I would never be a gifted performer. But because of her love of music, because of the years of lessons from Miss

192

Ermine, because of Dr. Bremen's class and my acquaintance with Byron, I would always love music.

* * *

Byron's musical career flourished. Grandma sent me clippings from *The Nashville Tennessean,* and the programs of various performances he had sent to her. He continued his teaching at the conservatory, at the same time travelling to other cities to play special concerts with well-known orchestras. He even sent me a recording of his recent organ recital at the National Cathedral in Washington, DC.

We kept in touch off and on over the years. I always recognized his letters by that thin, slanted handwriting on the envelope. Of course, I was back in town for vacations and family visits, but Byron wasn't. He had no family to visit there.

However, we *were* both there, about fifteen years later. Grandma had kept in close touch with his career, and when she died, he came back to play the music for her funeral.

Because of his tight schedule, we had no chance to talk before the service, but I made sure to arrive early so I could claim my favorite seat in the sanctuary, the place under the apex of the vaulted ceiling where stained-glassed streams of light and the organ's blended chords seemed to converge.

A taller Byron entered the loft and strode past the choir seats to the organ. He settled himself on the wooden bench and began pulling the stops, testing keys and pedals. Then he sat upright and played a few bars of music, made a couple of adjustments and launched into— *Beethoven's Ninth.* Of course, it would be *Beethoven!*

He sat tall, his back straight, even when his head, which was often turned to the side as if to listen, moved towards the keyboard. But what I immediately noticed was his hair. No longer trimmed close to the head, by his mother's scissors, but shoulder length and flaxen in the light of the organ lamp. Although I couldn't see his face, I knew the expression that would be there, one of intent listening, as though he could hear Beethoven breathing the notes through those tall brass pipes.

The congregation was absorbed also. Methodists are a chatty group, usually whispering to neighbors before the service, mouthing welcomes to friends across the aisle, gesturing and smiling hellos. There was none of that. Something special was happening, an uplift of spirit we were all caught in.

The service ended with the benediction, yet people were slow to stir until Byron launched into a slightly louder and more sprightly reprisal of the "Hymn to Joy" section of the symphony. With the church doors open, the sound must have carried half-way to Main Street.

But I was too caught up in the moment to move. I looked up at Byron, his strong back, his arms so in command of the sound. Our eyes seemed to meet briefly in the organ mirror. The sanctuary was empty now. All that remained was Byron, and me, and the music.